MURDER ON THE SAUGATUCK CHAIN FERRY

A Saugatuck Murder Mystery

by

G Corwin Stoppel

❖

Lord Hiltensweiller Press

THE SAUGATUCK MURDER MYSTERY SERIES

The Great Saugatuck Murder Mystery

Death by Palette Knife

A Murder of Crows

The Murder of the Saugatuck Yarn Hoarder

Murder on the Saugatuck Chain Ferry

ISBN: 9781095655399

In honor and appreciation of Ann —
lifelong friend, artist, and the inspiration for Beatrix.

Once again I am deeply indebted to two magnificent friends, Dr. Peter Schakel and John Thomas, who proof-read, edited, and went through several red ink pens - each. And to Sally Winters who has the uncanny ability to take a manuscript and convert it into a book. Above all, to my wife Pat for her encouragement over the months, and who endured the chatter of typewriter-app computer keys and countless hours of early jazz music while I wrote.

A very special thank you to Marilyn Starring and her family. Their boat, The Star of Saugatuck, *inspired the idea of* The Aurora. *Then, about a year ago she teasingly challenged me when she asked.* "*How would you murder someone on the Saugatuck Chain Ferry in the middle of the Kalamazoo River and still get away with it?*"

FORWARD

This is the fifth book in what has become the Saugatuck Murder Mystery Series. If you have not yet read *The Great Saugatuck Murder Mystery, Death by Palette Knife, A Murder of Crows* and *The Murder of the Saugatuck Yarn Hoarder* you might enjoy them. Many of the major characters were introduced in the first one; others came in the second. Like the other books, this story is set in Saugatuck, Michigan in the 1920s.

And, like the previous mysteries, this story is a absolute fiction, but don't let that stop you from enjoying it! The characters are complete works of fiction, and if you think otherwise, you are sadly mistaken. If you even think that there is some resemblance to a real person, living or dead, that is your imagination working over time.

— Spring 2019
  G Corwin Stoppel

CHAPTER ONE

For many years, until it was replaced by Venetian Night, and then expanded to Venetian Weekend, the Midsummer Festival had been Saugatuck's social highlight of the season. It was not, however, an event without considerable annual controversy. The area residents were almost evenly divided as to whether the celebration should be held on the eve of the longest day of the year or on the night of it. Each year there was a barrage of letters to the local paper, and the editor of the *Commercial Record* dutifully printed all of them. A few cynics even believed he was behind the great controversy, just for the sake of boosting revenues; others said the owners of the Big Pavilion were behind the debate, using it as free advertising.

That year, none of it seemed to matter. Fairy Nightshade was dead and buried, her reign of terror and threat of blackmail gone. She had taken all of her secrets with her to the grave. Word eventually spread that after a careful inspection of her house, there had been no written records, or, for that matter, much of anything else except yarn. There was a lot of yarn, and the news quickly converted anxiety to dry humour about her being a knit-wit. Even Chief Garrison, suspecting he might have been on her lists or among her records, was happy to spread the message that nothing had been found, and joked about all the yarns we could tell about her. As for the Mouse, even though most people felt sorry for her, no one really mourned when Doctor Landis drove her to a sanatorium. Everyone nodded in agreement that the bereavement of her one and only friend had clouded her mind, and that was why she shot Doctor Horace Balfour in the leg.

On the whole, Saugatuck was ready to celebrate the longest day of the year.

Two weeks before the big night there were signs and posters all over town announcing the return of the Blackhawk Orchestra from Aurora, Illinois, with Oliver Anderson as its leader and on the drums. Even though tickets had doubled in price that year, they were the hot ticket.

Doctor Horace sent Fred to the box office at the Big Pavilion the morning the tickets went on sale, and he had to wait in line for over half an hour. He bought ten tickets, and spent another twenty of his employer's dollars on a reserved table rather than open seating, then returned to the *Aurora* in triumph, smiling as he handed his employer the tickets and receipt.

Standing in line to buy tickets was not something Doctor Horace Balfour would have done in the best of times, and that early June was far from the best of times. The Mouse's bullet had barely grazed his leg, but he constantly howled and complained about the wound. "Horace, you are discrediting all physicians everywhere, merely proving the common belief that a doctor makes a terrible patient," Beatrix had told him sharply, but to no avail. His brother Theo agreed, reminding him that it was such a minor wound that during the war soldiers were patched up at an aid station, then sent right back to the front.

Every morning when Doctor Landis made his rounds, his first call was on Doctor Horace to check the wound and change the dressing. "I like to get the troublesome boy over and done with," he told Beatrix, and she smiled knowingly. Every afternoon Fred drove his boss a few blocks to what they both called his 'physical therapist' for an hour-long session. The exact type of physical therapy was a secret kept from the rest of his family and especially from Beatrix.

Even though Beatrix kept close watch over his recovery, she readily agreed when he insisted she spend time painting at Ox-Bow. She needed a break from him.

Horace was not the only creator and keeper of secrets. One Friday evening after Beatrix returned from her afternoon painting on the Ox-Bow meadow, Doctor Horace's sister-in-law, Clarice, announced that she and Beatrix, along with Harriet and Phoebe, were going into Chicago the next day. They would take the morning train into the city and come home late that night. When Theo, her husband, asked what they were doing, she sweetly smiled, and said that whatever the four women had planned was nobody's business. Horace said nothing, but from the expression on his face, it was obvious that he too was curious about their mysterious trip.

With all of these mysteries swirling about, the only thing everyone knew was that on Midsummer Night they would have a light supper of cold sandwiches on the *Aurora* and at ten minutes until eight would walk to the dance hall. Since Captain and Mrs. Garwood would be joining the rest of them, Horace had decided it wasn't fair to ask for a full dinner. He told them, "And, remember, we muster on the deck before seven fifty, not a minute later!"

Horace, Theo, and Fred, were ready first, and idly waiting in the library for the others. "Thunderation! I'm in the waiting room!" Horace had groaned every time he looked at his watch. Theo had long since given up reminding him to be patient. "Do you know the non-medical reason husbands die first?" Horace asked. "It's because it takes their wives so long to get ready to go anywhere." The joke was lost on Fred, a devout bachelor, who just looked confused, and finally piped up, "Guess I'll live forever then."

Theo answered, "I wouldn't mention that joke around Clarice or Beatrix if I were you. You might not tell that around Phoebe, either."

Captain and Mrs. Garwood were the next to arrive, holding hands as they walked across the deck, both of them in their best "Sunday going to meeting" clothes. "I believe, Captain, that is the first time I have seen you without your cap. I didn't know you still had so much hair," Theo quipped. Before he could answer, they heard Clarice call up the stairs, "Ready or not, here we come!"

She charged up the stairs, giggling, with Beatrix close behind, both wearing identical blue beaded dresses. "Now you see why we went to Chicago," Clarice giggled. "We wanted to be ready to 'Charleston back to Charleston' as they say in the song." She did a few dance steps, then swirled around. "Approve? It's the latest fashion. And the answer should probably be 'yes.'"

Clarice looked perfectly comfortable; Beatrix was just the opposite, trying to tug her dress down a half-inch lower. "I think the dress is terribly short and too revealing, especially for a woman of a certain age; my age in particular. I fear for my reputation," she told Horace, almost hoping he would agree so she could change into something more conservative.

"I think you look swell," he said, giving her a big smile. She tried to accept the compliment, but all she really wanted to do was hurry back to her cabin, lock the door behind her, and hide for the rest of the evening.

Before she had the chance to make her getaway they heard Harriet shout, "You-who!" as she and Phoebe came up the gangplank.

Mother and daughter stunned the others. They were wearing blue dresses that perfectly matched Clarice and Beatrix. More than that, they had bobbed their hair.

Clarice recovered quickly, and changed the topic from hair to frocks. "Great minds think along the same path, and blue is this year's color, you know!"

"Say, let's get going," Theo said loudly. "Don't want to miss a thing tonight." He turned to Clarice and added, "Got to show off my best girl."

They formed up in pairs, with Horace and Beatrix taking the lead. Next came Phoebe and Harriet, with Theo and Clarice behind them, and then the Garwoods. Fred was quite content to bring up the rear. When they started down Water Street, Phoebe was about to run forward to walk with her grandfather, but her mother held her back. "Not tonight, dear." Phoebe sulked but continued walking with her mother.

"I hope no one mistakes me for a libertine," Beatrix had anxiously whispered to Horace.

"Trust me, they won't. Just one very smart looking woman, fashionably dressed" he told her. "Blue is a good color for you; always has been. Besides, after what we've been through so far this summer, it's our turn to have some fun. And Beatrix, you aren't the only one with a surprise or two." For a moment or two Doctor Balfour had forgotten that Beatrix was never comfortable with surprises. He felt her stiffen and whispered to her, "I'm steady on my feet because I've taken physical therapy while you were at Ox-Bow."

"Oh! That is a good thing. Good."

Phoebe, walking behind her grandfather and Beatrix, was beginning to feel quite ill, and it had nothing to do with her health or her outfit. It was from watching the two of them walking so close to each other, and the way Beatrix would lean in to listen to something her grandfather was saying, and then smile at him. Worse, she was still holding his arm, when she must have perfectly known he was fully recovered and steady enough on his feet to walk without being protected. Phoebe was so angry and hurt she was ready to go home before they even got to the dance.

Her mood did not brighten when the band began playing the third song of the night, and Horace led Beatrix on to the dance floor. "Are you sure this is wise?" Beatrix asked.

"Absolutely not," he teased, catching the tempo and leading her into a foxtrot. She was surprised, and then delighted that he seemed to know what he was doing, as he led her around the floor with confidence. It alarmed her at first, and then she began to relax.

"Horace, just what type of physical therapy were you doing?" she asked.

"Well, it was a bit different; definitely not a medically recognized regimen. You see, to my way of thinking, learning a few dance steps seemed better than boring old exercises," he said, trying to brush it off.

"And, of course, it had nothing to do with the Midsummer party tonight, did it?" she asked.

"Why, of course not!" he answered, then winked.

A lump in her throat made it nearly impossible for Beatrix to say what she was feeling.

Horace and Beatrix stayed on the dance floor through the rest of the first twenty-minute set, then joined the others at their table. "Pretty fancy moves, big brother. Clifton Webb and his sister had better watch out if you two ever get to Hollywood," Theo told him. "You're to be congratulated for the way you let Beatrix lead,"

"I did not lead!" Beatrix said quickly. "I believe Horace has hidden talents. Phoebe, perhaps you would enjoy a dance with your grandfather."

Phoebe smiled. She had long since lost her fondness for Beatrix, but a chance to reclaim her grandfather from the clutches of *that woman* was not to be missed. She smiled, and agreed. When the band started, Horace held out his hand and said, "Just follow my lead," he told her over the sound of the music. After the second tune she asked, "One more?" and smiled again when he agreed. After each tune, Phoebe would ask, "Just one more?"

It was only when the band took their second break that the two returned to the table. Beatrix quickly agreed with Horace that the two of them were ready to call it a night and leave. "The noise is quite intense, is it not?" Beatrix asked once they were outside. "Perhaps a quiet walk will be a better way of celebrating the shortest night of the year."

It was very late by the time they returned to the *Aurora*.

CHAPTER TWO

When Bob Campbell came home for the summer after his second year at the University of Chicago, he immediately went back to work cranking the chain ferry back and forth across the Kalamazoo River. It was the same summer job he'd had since he was a freshman in high school, and he had a reputation for being a "steady worker." He was paid reasonably well, and several years earlier learned the *real* money was in the tips from the passengers. Tell a few stories, let a youngster take a few cranks on the handle, and shoot the breeze with their folks, and the tips added up. Impress them that the ferry had been in operation for almost eighty years, flash a smile, maybe even gently flirt with some of the older women passengers, and most days he made three or four times more money in tips than salary.

For the most part he liked the job. To an outsider, it looked like mindless hard work, but Bob knew he had to watch the current and the other boats going up and down the river while he crossed. A few hotshot boaters tried to get as close as possible to the ferry, hoping to make a hard turn and spray the passengers, not realizing they could get hung up on the chain just beneath the surface. He had a sixth sense for them and kept his megaphone close at hand to order them to keep their distance.

Sometimes, the passengers were the challenge. Every summer, especially on the weekends, Bob could count on having a few men and women, mostly college boys, who had been drinking hard. Once in a great while some angry young man would turn surly and ready to throw a punch; but most of them were jovial and good-natured.

The worst of them were the dare devils. About once a week a young man with a group of friends would suddenly get off the ferry just as they ready to leave. Bob knew what was coming. The fellow would strip down to his BVDs, or even less, toss his clothes and shoes on the boat and shout, "See you on the other side!" At least they weren't as dumb as the passengers who would suddenly stand on the ferry's supply box halfway across the river, jump in, and try to swim the rest of the way. It was a fool-hardy thing to do in the fast current, and there was always the chance one of them would get pulled under and drown. Every few years a body was pulled out of the river.

As much as Bob enjoyed the summer job, he was always tired by the last crossing about six o'clock in the evening, and even later on Friday and Saturday night. Nothing was better than nights when no one was on the opposite shore waiting for him and he could tie off the ferry, snap the padlock on the supply box, and go home five or ten minutes early. He considered it a bonus. A few years earlier his mother had anxiously watched from the front parlor window to see him come home safe and sound. Now, she eagerly awaited the day he would come home to freshen up, then tell her that he'd be a bit late because he had met a nice girl and was walking out with her. She worried that he was working too much to allow himself any time for fun. Saving money for college was admirable, and she was grateful he helped with the household expenses without being asked, but she didn't think it would hurt for him to splurge once in a while and treat a nice girl to a parfait at the drugstore. The truth of the matter was, after a long day, especially a sunny and hot one, all Bob wanted to do was go home, freshen up, and go to bed.

On an unseasonably warm Saturday evening in early July, Bob's luck didn't hold out. He had just brought the ferry back to the little wharf in Saugatuck when he saw lights flashing and heard a car horn tooting on the opposite shore. "Bridge is closed," the driver shouted across the water. Bob dutifully cranked the ferry across the river. The car was a big Buick, what many of his friends called a "doctor's car," so he hoped that a generous tip would make it all worthwhile.

"Bridge is out," the driver repeated as Bob came closer to the dock.

"Happens sometimes. It's old. Sometimes it won't lock into place like it should. Good thing you got here when you did . Two minutes later and I'd be off duty," he smiled. He didn't bother to explain that they could have driven down along the lakeshore a few miles, turned around, then turned up a county road and made their way back to Saugatuck. Bob instructed the driver how to pull the car onto the ferry deck, and asked him to put the chocks behind the rear wheels, while he put them in front of the front tires. "Ready? You got it in gear?" he asked.

The driver seemed friendly enough and came over to the side of the ferry where Bob was pulling on the crank. For the next few minutes they made the typical tourist small talk: weather, the Big Pavilion, boats tied up for the night. They watched as someone along the shore lit a skyrocket and it arched into the sky. His passenger said he worked for a man who owned a flower shop on the north side of Chicago as a second rocket raced upward, and burst with a shower of sparks, followed a few second later by the boom from the explosion. "Fools," Bob said. "Probably too gassed to know the sun is still up." His passenger laughed.

When they got to the Saugatuck-side of the river, the driver gave Bob a ten spot as a tip. Bob thanked him, relieved that the final trip was worth the effort.

The only thing that seemed a bit odd was that when Bob was ready to lock up the boat, the supply box was already locked. "Must have done it before I picked them up," he said out loud. It didn't matter. It was late, he was tired, and he was going to have to get up early the next day. He yawned and walked home, glad the day was over.

Just as he did every night, he emptied his pockets of coins and bills into a small pile on the dining room table. He took a dollar and some change for himself, then pushed the rest of it across to his mother to help with expenses. The rest of it went into the bank for tuition and room and board. "I'm not touching a penny of that money, young man. When you get into Chicago I want you to have a good time. And you see to it that you treat your friends to a red hot or something. Peanuts, Cracker Jacks, it doesn't matter to me. I didn't raise you to be a piker. You take that money. All of it," she told him.

Bob knew better than to argue with his mother. He agreed, but tucked half of it into his sock drawer. He'd give it to her the next night when he came from work. Then he changed his mind and decided to keep the ten dollar bill, justifying it in case of an emergency.

CHAPTER THREE

For several days after the Midsummer gala at the Big Pavilion, Phoebe had moped around the house, in abject misery. Even if her grandfather had danced with her, she could feel that Beatrix had become an increasingly important part of his life. It wasn't just the dance. She knew they had slipped away for a long walk that night, and feared what that might lead to. Just before school ended for the summer, a girl who was just a year older than her had whispered she'd gone out for a walk with a boy and they had snuggled on a bench. And that wasn't all - they'd kissed! Phoebe was sure Beatrix would try to kiss her grandfather! More and more she had seen them talking with each other, or sometimes just sitting next to each other on the deck and not even talking. It wasn't that she and her grandfather were growing apart, but more that their lives were changing. She wanted life to be the way it had been that first summer when she had him all to herself.

When Phoebe's mother asked her daughter how she knew Beatrix had become a wedge, Phoebe responded with a phrase she had heard from others, "Woman's intuition."

For a few moments Harriet said nothing. Her daughter was right. Ever since Beatrix had flown into their lives, it had changed all of the relationships. There were times when she felt exactly like Phoebe. If only Beatrix would just get into her plane and fly away.

"I see. You might be right. What do you think we can do about it?" Harriet asked. Phoebe didn't have an answer.

"Well, I have been thinking. We know that your grandfather enjoys reading the Sherlock Holmes mysteries, don't we? You could start there. Start reading the stories, and if you have questions, then ask him to explain it to you. Nothing makes a man feel better about himself than when he can explain things to a woman," Harriet told her.

"What do I do when I've read all the stories and run out of questions?" Phoebe asked.

"Dear, that will be a very long time coming. I don't think you need to worry about that! Besides, if you do run out of Sherlock Holmes, there are other mystery writers, like that new one, Agatha Christie. Oh, there is an even newer one named Dorothy Sayers. You might like reading her, too. If you read them first then you could tell your grandfather about her. So, what do you think? Worth trying, isn't it?"

Phoebe thought about it for a few minutes, then said, "I thought you told me women should stand on their own two feet."

"Of course, women should. Sometimes it just takes a little scheming to get what we want," her mother answered. "And, your aunt Clarice told me that Beatrix received a telegram asking her to fly to Indianapolis to look at a painting! She'll be gone for several days, so I think now is your chance."

"Then, I'll go right over to the *Aurora* and ask Grandfather if I can read one of his mysteries!"

"You might start by asking his advice on which story you should read first. Remember what I said about getting him to explain things to you. Sometimes a step backward leads to two steps forward."

"Mother, do you think Beatrix asks him to explain things?"

Harriet pursed her lips. "I doubt it. So, that's to your advantage."

Half an hour later Phoebe was sitting on a deck chair next to her grandfather reading *The Adventure of the Blue Carbuncle.* He was reading the day old newspaper from Chicago.

Even an amateur junior detective like Phoebe could tell that he wasn't *really* reading the paper because he hadn't turned a page for a quarter hour. "Grandfather, something is on your mind," Phoebe suggested quietly.

He folded up the paper, then took off his glasses and put them in the breast pocket of his blazer. "Very perceptive of you, young lady. Yes. Yes, there is."

"Are you worried that Doctor Howell is all right?"

"She can look after herself, but yes, I suppose I am. She's an expert pilot and if she gets into a jam she'll know what to do. She's no stunt pilot. Still...."

"And you'll be restless until she gets back, won't you?"

"Well, perhaps not that long. She promised to send a telegram when she gets there. And another one when she is coming back. So, that's something, I guess," he told her.

Phoebe didn't dare to ask if he was lonely without Beatrix.

Nor did her grandfather tell her everything that was on his mind. It was something that his brother Theo had said a few minutes before Phoebe stepped onto the boat.

"You know, Horace, I'm happy for you. I want you to know that; you deserve it. Look, I'm not fond of that woman, but if you're happy, well, that's what I want for you. I just want you to think about something."

"What's that?"

"Well, it's more about you than anything else. Look, it's been ten years since, well, ten years that you've been alone. You're cantankerous, impatient, and set in your ways. Sometimes you are impossibly arrogant. I know you enjoy being with her, but if this turns serious, you might have to loosen up. Well, at least a little."

"Thunderation! I am not cantankerous, impatient, or set in my ways! It's just that I've learned how to take care of myself!" Horace snapped at him.

"Well, be that as it may. Let's just say that you're your own best friend when you're not your own worst enemy. My guess is Beatrix's set in her ways, being single all these years. Besides, there's more to think about than that," Theo said, trying to cool down his brother.

"What?" Horace demanded.

"Horace, you're the finest surgeon I know, and I'm not just saying that because you're my brother. It's the truth. As much as I hate to encourage you on these detective adventures of yours, you turned out to be a natural at it. But when it comes to understanding people, what makes them tick, feelings, and things like that, well, I hate to say it, but you are a rank amateur."

"Thunderation! I am not. I'm as caring as the next man!"

"Right," Theo said with sarcasm. "Let me ask you something. Now you and Beatrix have been chumming around for the better part of two years, and you're still more like brother and sister than anything else."

"We just aren't affectionate in public," Horace said slowly.

"That's fine. But you aren't in public all the time. This morning, you drove her out to the airfield to see her off. Just the two of you. No one else around. Did it even cross your mind to give her a kiss good-bye?"

"That's rather personal," Horace finally said. He twisted uncomfortably in his chair.

"You don't need to answer the question. Keep it to yourself, for all I care. My hunch is you didn't, and she didn't look at you all dewy-eyed hoping you would take the initiative. When it comes to being icy, you two are a perfect match. Sometimes when either of you walks into a room the temperature drops. But I want you to think about this while Beatrix is gone. You two continue keeping each other company, and well, let's just say get serious about each other as a couple, and then you end up getting married..."

Horace held up his hand to stop his brother. "You're rushing things a bit, aren't you? I don't think of her that way, and I'm sure she doesn't think that way either!"

"I don't believe you just said that! I know the war has been over for ten years, and you're not rushing into some war time romance and marriage before you go off to fight the Hun, but be reasonable! It's been two years, and if it does happen, well, think ahead, big brother. What are you planning? A good night handshake and head off to separate bedrooms and have breakfast together the next morning?"

"Now, listen up. You're rushing ahead of yourself! Your imagination is getting the best of you. Clarice put you up to this?" Horace asked angrily.

"No, she didn't. I thought of it all on my own! Like I said, I'm not fond of her, but I don't want to see either of you get hurt. All I'm asking is you give some thought to what I said because when it comes to being affectionate you are at the bottom of the class." Theo got up from his chair, turned and said, "I'm walking into town. Stretch my legs."

Horace watched him walk down the gangplank and step on to the sidewalk. He returned to his opened newspaper, but he couldn't read. He was angry with his brother, and at the same time, knew he was right. Partially right. Maybe more than just partially right. Or perhaps completely out of line and wrong.

For a diversion, Phoebe's timing could not have been better. There was something on his mind, but he didn't want to face it. Nor was he about to discuss it with her. He changed the subject and asked, "What say you and I walk down to the first fish shack we find and buy a nice mess of whitefish for Mrs. Garwood to cook up for tonight?" he asked her.

"Walk? Who is carrying the fish back home?" she asked, squinting her eyes

"We'll drive then. We'll get some fish and give them to Mrs. Garwood. Then what say I teach you how to drive?"

"Drive? I don't know how to drive, and Mother said I'm not old enough to learn."

"Thunderation! I was driving at your age, and before that had a horse and buggy. In that case your first lesson should be in the cemetery. That's where your uncle Theo and I learned how to drive."

"Because," she said slowly, "If we have an accident and get killed we'll be closer to where we'll be going?"

"No. Because there's not much traffic and everyone drives very slowly at a cemetery, and the roads are narrow and short. You can learn how to turn and back up, and that's better than out on a street."

Phoebe thought it through and smiled, "Jake with me! Just promise that we bring the fish back here first so they don't stink up the car."

"No danger in forgetting. Definitely." Horace was close to flashing a smile.

CHAPTER FOUR

"You still haven't told your mother about learning how to drive, have you?" Horace asked Phoebe on the fourth morning of her lessons.

"No, and I think it's a secret we should keep to ourselves," she answered as she slid behind the steering wheel. "Okay, clutch in and the transmission should be in first gear, right? Ready for me to turn the key?" she asked.

"Ready! Now remember, put your right foot lightly on the gas pedal so you don't stall out, and then gently let up on the clutch." After two days of either lurching forward or stalling, she was finally getting her coordination right. That morning it had come after just three stalls that had almost made her tear up in frustration. Horace held his breath as she tried again. She took a deep breath, her fingers grasping the wheel, then reaching forward with her right hand to turn the key.

"Perfect! Even Fred couldn't do it any better and he's the best there is. Now, let's just drive around slowly and practice making your turns. We'll keep it in first gear for a few times. And remember, when you make a left turn, hold your arm straight out the window; right turn, bend your elbow into an 'L'. Now, this is the important part: no matter how good you get, no watching for boys and waving to them. Concentrate on what you are doing," he said sternly.

To his delight, his granddaughter was an excellent student. They spent about half an hour on the gravel roads at Riverside Cemetery, and then Horace said it was time to go back to the boat. "Just a few more minutes," she pleaded.

"No. Not today. I've got to do something important this morning," he told her.

They changed places so he could drive them back into town. "See you later," he said when he stopped in front of the gangplank.

A few minutes later she heard an airplane overhead, and knew where he was going. The roar got louder, and in a minute she could see Beatrix's bright yellow biplane flying up over the Kalamazoo River, heading for the airfield. As she approached the *Aurora* she wiggle-waggled the wings as a greeting. "She's back," she muttered in disgust. Phoebe wanted to cross her fingers and hope that Beatrix would land safely, but she couldn't bring herself to do it.

Horace leaned against his car at the far end of the grassy field, waiting for Beatrix to land and taxi into place. He was trying to convince himself that he should give her a welcome-home hug, maybe even a quick kiss, just on a cheek, and tell her that he missed her. But what if she didn't want to be hugged, much less kissed? He could ruin everything. The first time he had given her a quick hug she had stiffened up. Maybe she would this time, too. But then again, what if she would welcome a token of affection, he wondered. And would she be disappointed if he didn't do something?

She had seen him, of course, and when she turned off the engine and waited for the propeller to quit turning, she smiled and waved at him. That was encouraging, he thought. She was happy to see him. Horace quickly decided he would give her a hug and maybe a quick light kiss on the cheeks, like the French did during the war when an aviator landed in one piece. As he walked toward her, he could see her remove her goggles and leather helmet, and shake out her hair.

"You might want to stay up wind of me," she said. He looked at her face, noticing that it was covered with residue from the exhaust.

"What happened? Are you all right?" he asked.

"I am fine, and before you ask, so is my plane. I am certain I look horrible," she apologized flatly.

"What happened?"Horace repeated.

"A very unpleasant former Air Corp corporal working at the Indianapolis airfield made it very clear that he does not believe a woman is capable of flying an aeroplane, and then informed me that women should not be allowed to fly. I assure you, he was very rigid in his opinions and expressed them at volume. When he filled the tanks, I believe he added a quart or two of oil. From the taste and smell, I believe it was castor oil."

"Thunderation!" Horace bellowed.

"I quite agree. My language was quite explicit and very unlady-like. I have experienced that sort of attitude before, and I do not like it. However, putting oil in the tank was something dangerously unacceptable," Beatrix said calmly.

"What happened?" Horace asked for the third time.

"I took off and once in the air the engine coughed a few times, and there was black smoke. I could smell that it was oil, and my first thought was that a piston ring was leaking. I gained altitude in case I had to turn back to land, and enriched the fuel to air ratio which resolved the worst of the problem. It still coughed a few times as I crossed into Michigan which is why I look rather unbecoming. And I had to fly higher than I like in case the engine stalled out and I needed to find a place to put it down."

"Glide, you mean?"

"Exactly. A dead-stick landing, and it is a dangerous manoeuvre. Horace, I do not wish to complain, but I am filthy, I reek of exhaust and oil, and I am very cold. Would it be inconvenient to take me directly back to the *Aurora* so I can take my ablutions?" she asked. "I will get my flight bag first."

"Right away. You can tell me about the rest of your adventures on the ground later," Horace replied. He offered his hand to steady her across the grass, but she ignored the gesture. She was in too feisty a mood to allow him to carry her bag, but kind enough not to snap at his offer.

When they got aboard the boat, she turned to him. "Thank you for coming out to the airfield to get me. I will see you at dinner." She started down the stairs to her cabin, stopped to turn around. "Horace, thank you for always being a perfect gentleman."

"If you're up for it, stop by my library before dinner for a little antifreeze," Horace smiled. "It might warm you up."

She ignored his offer as she walked to her cabin.

"I trust I am interrupting," Beatrix smiled as she came into the library. "Please tell me I have not missed the first dinner gong."

"No, plenty of time. What's your poison?" Horace asked.

"Please, Horace, considering some of our adventures, that is a very unfortunate choice of words. If it is Scotch you are imply-ing, however, a small one would be most welcome, with an equal amount of water."

"Tell me about your adventures on the ground," Horace said as he handed her a glass.

"It was very interesting. A very nice man, an engineer, and his wife moved into his parent's home after they passed away. To make a long story short, his father had been a lieutenant colonel in the Marine Corp and purchased some paintings in Paris just after the Armistice. After the colonel died, the son inherited the paintings, and wanted to know if they were worth keeping."

"Were they?" Horace asked, leaning closer.

"Not now. Perhaps some day, but only after the artists pass away. Duffy, Raoul Duffy, that is, is doing his best to drink himself into an early grave, but Matisse is going strong. Paintings do not become truly valuable until the artist is dead. A very sad fact, and one that I believe is often forgotten by my fellow painters at Ox-Bow. Sylvia and Cora are very talented young artists, but I fear that will be taken for granted as long as they are alive. Honored, perhaps, but not valued."

"Too bad," Horace said.

"And what about you? Any great adventures?"

"Just that I spent some time with Phoebe. We, ah well, it's supposed to be a secret, at least a secret from her mother, but...."

Beatrix cut him off with a wave of the hand. "If it is a secret then you must not tell me."

He gave her a half-smile, and they lapsed into silence until Mrs. Garwood rang the gong calling them to dinner. He noticed Beatrix trying to stifle a yawn.

Almost immediately after dinner she excused herself from the table. "I hope you will forgive me, but it has been a very arduous day. Good night, all."

Horace looked a bit glum as she went to her cabin. "Cheer up, big brother," Theo whispered, leaning closer. "You missed the bullet tonight."

"What do you mean?"

"You didn't have to talk with her. Remember our earlier conversation? You missed the bullet."

"Thunderation!" Horace said as he stalked off to his library.

Harriet dropped her daughter off at the ship a little after eight the next morning. A few minutes later she was settled into a deck chair, trying to make sense of a Sherlock Holmes mystery, sitting quietly next to her grandfather who was reading an article in the *Chicago Tribune*. She had looked up from the book and noticed several cars hurrying down Water Street to the chain ferry.

"Grandfather, something's happening over at the ferry. All of a sudden there are a couple of cars there, and I see Chief Garrison talking to some men."

He put down his paper to look down the river, then said, "Probably someone tried stealing something, or maybe a little vandalism." He returned to his paper, oblivious that Phoebe had gone up to the bow of the ship for a better look.

Neither of them noticed Doctor Landis as he sped past, but he had spotted them. The young doctor did a u-turn at the intersection of Water and Main Streets and pulled up in front of the *Aurora*. "Horace! Need you to come along with me. Something bad at the ferry. I just got the call."

Horace was on his feet in a flash, more than eager for a diversion and excitement. "Phoebe! My bag is in the study. Go and get it for me, then hurry and meet me down on the street," he commanded.

She quickly obeyed, hoping that she would be invited along, and all the more so since there had been no sign of Beatrix lurking about. The girl was elated. She wasn't just going to read about adventures, she was going to get her chance to be Doctor John Watson to her grandfather's Sherlock Holmes. Even better, to her delight, Horace didn't tell her to stay on the boat.

"Where's Doc Howell this morning?" Landis asked as he held open the rear door for them.

"No sign of her yet. You think we need her?"

For a moment Phoebe was anxious that her grandfather would tell her to go back on the boat and find Beatrix. She held her breath, relieved when Horace said, "Let's see what this is all about first. We can always fetch her later if she's needed to attend." Phoebe would have her grandfather all to herself, and on a mystery, perhaps even an adventure worthy of Sherlock Holmes himself.

A gentle breeze was blowing across the river. All three of them sniffed the air as they got out of the car. "That's a bit ripe," Horace said. "Let's hope it's an animal." He turned to Phoebe. "All right young lady, much as we could use a good first assistant, this isn't the place for you right now. I want you to stay by the car. Stay right there so I can spot you. If we need Beatrix or your uncle Theo, I'll give you a big wave. You run back to the boat and get them. And get Fred to bring down the car. Jake with you?"

"Jake," she agreed. It wasn't the assignment she wanted, but it left her with the hope that nothing would ever change between the two of them. She'd always be his best girl. She watched with pride as her grandfather hurried with Doctor Landis to the ferry.

"Definitely ripe," Horace observed as he and the town physician walked quickly along the gravel path. "Any idea who that is with Chief Garrison?"

"That's Mac. I don't know his last name. Everyone just calls him 'Mac'. He bought the ferry business a couple of years back. Good man, but watch out, he can be a bit rough around the edges. Phoebs might learn some new words they don't teach in school."

The police chief and a deputy were standing on the ferry, looking down at Mac on his knees, trying to unlock the storage box. "What I can't figure out is why this key doesn't work," he growled, trying the padlock yet again. "I know it's the right key, that's for sure."

"Maybe think someone switched locks on you?" the chief asked. "Whatever is in there has been dead for a while."

"You're sure right about that, Chief," his deputy said. "I'll betcha some kid cut the old lock and put some ground beef or something like that in there. That's what I'm thinking. Maybe a dead cat or rat or something."

"I don't care what you're thinking. We've gotta get it open and find out. Try a different key. Maybe you're using the wrong one."

"Chief, I used every key on the ring, and I'm telling you, this is the right one. I ought to know my own keys. Someone's done changed the lock on me!" Mac retorted.

"Then get out of my way and I'll shoot it off!" the chief bellowed, unsnapping the strap on his holster.

"Hold on just a second," Doctor Balfour said quietly. "Let me try opening it." He rummaged through his black bag and found a set of dental tools.

"What are you doing with burglar tools! That's against the law, you carrying them. I could run you in for that," the chief snapped.

"These are dental tools. Only in this case, they can serve another purpose, so quit your fussing! Thunderation, you want this opened, don't you?" Horace bent over the box, tinkered with two tools he inserted into the lock, and was rewarded with a satisfying snap as it sprung open. He stood up and smiled in triumph. "Done, and not a single ricochet in town." He stepped back so the chief and his deputy could open the box. The stench was over-whelming, and Horace instantly pulled the red pocket square from his jacket pocket.

"Dead body, and I figure he's been that way for a while," the chief whispered, stating the very obvious.

Horace turned around to face Phoebe, and put four fingers into his mouth to whistle at her. As she ran towards him, he quickly walked in her direction, stopping her before she got too close. "Go back to the boat and get Fred, and if you see my brother and Doctor Howell, better bring them along, too. Tell Fred to bring the car, and bring me my walking stick while you're there. The one with the silver head. Now, go!" He watched as she sprinted the three blocks down the street, intentionally taking his time before returning to the ferry.

"You can't leave him there!" Max shouted hotly when the chief and his deputy laid the deceased man on a canvas spread on the deck of the boat. "I got a business to run, and I'm not hauling passengers with a body on board. Move him over to the grass or somewhere else!"

"The body stays here for the time-being until I give the okey-doke to move it. Listen up, you're not going anywhere on this ferry until I say so. Maybe not until tomorrow or the day after. And you're going to stay right here on this boat until I get some information out of you. This fellow's been murdered, and that makes this an official crime scene. Now you pipe down or I'll run you in for interfering with police business," the chief told him.

"What makes you so sure it's murder?" Mac asked, protesting the potential lost revenue.

"On account of the fact that he's dead, and a stiff doesn't just decide to come onto your boat, stretch himself out here in the box like it's his coffin, lock himself in, and wait for us to come find him. Somebody put him in there, dead or alive, and that makes it suspicious enough right then and there. It might be murder or not, but one thing's for sure. You're not moving this ferry until I say you can move it. And you're staying put, too. That clear?"

Mac pushed a worn brown fedora back on his head and ran the right sleeve of his shirt across his brow. "Yeah, I can see your point. Makes sense, but you're still taking money out of my pocket leaving him there like that. And it doesn't seem respectful."

The chief ignored him and turned to Horace to ask, "Balfour, that lady doctor friend of yours - you send for her, yet?"

"Doctor Howell will be here soon," he said.

"Yeah, good. Much as I hate to admit it, for a woman, she's got brains. We'll probably need her. Landis, I figure that when we finish up here we'll take the body to the hospital so you can figure out how he got himself killed."

Doctor Landis turned toward Horace. "Thank goodness for the new ventilation fans. We'll want them turned on high when we do the post-mortem. Horace, look, as for what the chief said about Doctor Howell. Forget it. That woman has got more brains than you, I, and your brother Theo put together. Glad she'll be with us. No matter what the chief thinks, I want you to know it."

Horace smiled in appreciation. "You and I both." He chuckled, "Thunderation! And, I'm just smart enough to know that you're right."

While the two physicians waited for Phoebe, Fred, and Beatrix to arrive, Garrison began questioning Mac. He wanted a list of all his employees who had access to the storage box and lock, and the names of those who had worked for the past few days.

"Well, let's see, Tommy Avery was supposed to work yesterday, but he and his family had to drive over to Lansing for his aunt's funeral. See, it's like this - it's Tommy who usually fills in when Bob can't be here, so I had to hire some young fellow who talked about how he wanted a job. Well, he lasted about one round trip," Mac explained.

"When was that?" the chief asked. "Why'd he quit on you, or did you fire him? Who was he? I want his name!"

"Yesterday morning, first thing, about half past nine or so. He said he'd be here at nine, but he never showed until half an hour later. Let me tell you, when a fellow turns up that late I know they're no good. I showed him what he was supposed to do, and rode over and back with him, and then, without a single word, he just walked off the boat and kept going. Can you beat that? Can you?"

"And this fellow has a name, I take it?" the chief asked.

"Yeah, but I never quite caught it," Mac said.

His voice dripping with sarcasm, the chief replied, "That's a big help. You better try to remember his name. I want to talk with him. I'll bet it isn't every day some fellow comes up wanting a job on the chain ferry and walks off before he starts. That's suspicious. I need his name. So tell me, where was Bob Campbell that he couldn't work?"

"Oh, he and a couple of his buddies from school went into Chicago to see the Cubs."

"Right in the middle of summer, you let him go skylarking off like that?" the chief asked.

"Yeah, that's right, I sure did! Look, you know Bob. He's a good fellow. After his pa died he took care of his mother and finished up school. Most fellows would have dropped out to take a job. But he stuck with it, and a few of us chipped in to help him pay for college. Soon as he's done for the summer, he's right back here and working the next morning. He's going to make something of himself. You can just tell he's got ambitions; he's a steady worker. The way I figure it, it's good for him to have some clean fun with his friends once in a while. He'll be back today and here first thing in the morning. No doubt about it."

"Well, it's rather suspicious that the moment he goes off, one fellow runs off and you get one quitter on you, and Bob's gone when this fellow gets himself killed and locked in that box with a new lock on it. Real suspicious. I want to talk to him the moment he gets back. And I'd better not have to go down to Chicago to go looking for him, either!"

"Not when you have friends in low places to do the hunting for you," Landis whispered under his breath to Horace.

"You mean Capone?"

"About as low as you can get."

It was just under a quarter of an hour before Phoebe returned with Fred and Beatrix. Even before Fred turned off the engine, the girl was out of the car, running towards her grandfather, holding up his cane. Beatrix and Fred followed. Horace smiled when he saw Beatrix, relieved that she was obviously rested after her miserable flight from Indianapolis.

Phoebe handed him his walking stick. "I brought you the silver-headed one, like you asked, just in case you were facing danger or something," she said, proud of her selection from the collection of walking sticks in his library.

"Good. Thank you. Always best to be prepared." He held her hand while he talked with Fred. "I'd like to take Phoebe and the car to the boat. We've got some business here she doesn't need to see. No, better yet, I want you to drive down to Pier Cove or somewhere, and get some fresh fruit. Blueberries, watermelon, anything you can think of. And take your time," Horace said.

"Something up, General?" he asked.

"Garrison is going to want to move a body to the hospital. And before he gets any bright idea about saving a nickel's worth of gas by using my car, get it out of here. Go to Pier Cove. Go to South Haven if you have to. Just get my car out of here, and take Phoebs with you."

"Yes, Sir! That's right good thinking on your part, on account of the fact that I can tell from here that fellow has been out in no man's land too long. I remember our ambulances stunck to high heaven when we were fighting the Hun. That brings back some bad memories. We'll get on the road toot and sweet," Fred said. "Don't you worry. I'll keep Miss Phoebe out of this."

It was half past ten before Garrison allowed the doctors to remove the body to an ambulance. "You find anything, anything at all, you let me know!" he told them as they got into Doctor Landis's car.

When the body was laid out on the examination table, and three of them were scrubbed, gowned, and masked, Horace and Doctor Landis both wanted Beatrix to take the lead. She agreed, and turning to the two physicians and Doctor Landis' secretary, began. "From experience I have learned to always begin by making a close observation of the deceased's shoes. Their condition will reveal much about his life, work, and personality.

"Our John Doe is wearing expensive black wing-tip shoes. The leather is soft, relatively thin, and of high quality. From that, we can safely assume that he was a city dweller. Black, not brown, is worn in a city. The heals are not run-down, which indicates that he had good balance and a steady gait, suggesting that he was a man of confidence. Now, notice that the leather sole is beginning to show signs of wear under the balls of his feet. Both left and right are evenly matched. A sidewalk was his usual terrain, which is further evidence he lived and walked mostly in a large city. where he would walk Note also that the laces are even, not lopsided, which is an indication he was almost fastidious about his dress. Finally, they are well polished. The shoes are not new, but well cared-for. Please note that, as it may be beneficial to interview any of the shoeshine boys in town."

"All that from a pair of shoes!" Dr. Landis let out a soft whistle. "She is good."

"The best," Horace said quietly, smiling with pride behind his mask.

Beatrix continued. "You will observe that the deceased is in remarkably good physical condition. I believe he has been regular in taking exercise. And, we also see that he is nattily dressed. Perhaps something of a male peacock hoping to garner the attention of women. She paused to open his jacket to reveal a Brooks Brothers label. "A very expensive suit, with his tie from the same haberdashery. Notice also that his hair was recently cut, and he is freshly shaven. From the absence of small hairs on the collar, it was done more than a day before his death, but not more than two or three days."

Beatrix turned to the secretary. "Please make a side note to make inquiries at the local barbershops."

She turned again to the examination table. "Although we do not have hard evidence, we can safely assume that he is a visitor here.

Therefore, all things considered, it would not surprise me if he had aspirations of meeting a young woman. Notice the fresh crease in his trousers." She turned once more to the secretary to make sure she was writing down her observations. Beatrix carefully inspected the cuffs of his trousers. "As I thought, his shoes were polished the day he died." She pointed to a tiny dab of wax.

"Well done, Beatrix," Horace said.

She didn't respond, but stared silently at the body. "Would one of you please loosen his tie, remove it, and open up his shirt?"

Doctor Landis stepped forward remaining silent, waiting for Beatrix to continue. "You will notice it is a half-Windsor Knot, not a four-in-hand. As a young boy he was probably sent to a private school, perhaps a military school or academy. The half-Windsor is a favorite among young men because it is far easier to tie than the more traditional four-in-hand. It is an unfortunate habit some men carry into adult life. Please make a note of the type of knot," she told the secretary as she moved to the head of the table and stood silently as she observed everything.

"Now, this is interesting," she barely whispered excitedly when she turned his head to the left. "Notice the small blood stain on the right side of his collar. Although he is freshly shaven, this is not the work of a shaving blade. That would have been a nick. And if we look carefully, we find a small puncture wound just above the carotid artery. And, note that there is a slight bruise. That, gentlemen, barring any other evidence tells us how he was murdered. Someone used a rather large hypodermic needle."

"Poison?" Horace asked.

"Perhaps," she said flatly. "That would be the most common cause of death with an injection."

"Any hypotheses, Doctor Howell?" Doctor Landis asked.

Beatrix gave him a withering look. "The lab work on his blood will reveal if it is poison, and the type. We cannot allow ourselves the pleasure of speculation now. There are poisons from Asia which are almost impossible to diagnose. A compound made from ordinary tobacco leaves, soaked and then distilled would be lethal in even the most minute amounts. For that matter, plain ordinary room air, injected into an artery can lead to a fatal stroke within seconds."

"That's a bit far-fetched, don't you think?" Landis asked.

"Statistically, yes. The number of murders by that method is very rare. I have seen only one other case similar to this. It was a nurse, in October 1911, who killed her husband using a needle she stole from the hospital to create an embolism. From what I remember, he was a brutal man who beat her on a number of occasions, so she probably believed he had it coming. Still, pre-meditated murder remains murder, and she was sent to prison for life. That is why it is a dangerous course to make any speculations until we receive the lab reports."

Horace blew the air out of his cheeks. "Either way, if that's what happened here, someone must have known what they were doing. I'm betting on poison. Meanwhile, we don't know the deceased's name. Let's go through his pockets once more, just to be sure we didn't miss anything."

"I find the cause of death far more interesting than his identity," Beatrix said quietly.

"I understand, but let's check again," Landis reminded her.

"Gentlemen, there is one other place where men have been known to secret valuables. I would prefer one of you would check." She nodded at his belt. "Meanwhile, I will examine his shoes." Her suddenly modesty surprised Landis. Horace understood. In her own laboratory she would not have been so hesitant; with men present, she was being discreet.

Landis and Horace found nothing. Beatrix had better success. "I believe we know his name. Johnston Murphy," she said in triumph, holding up his right shoe.

"Beatrix, you might want to keep looking. Johnston Murphy is the name of the manufacturer," Horace said gently, grateful for the surgical mask which hid his smile.

"How embarrassing. Ah, Charlie Haggerty, according to the name stamped on the underside of the left shoe tongue," she said quietly. "Please forgive my previous mistake. I am not familiar with the manufacturer of shoes for men."

"And that gives us the 'who' and a partial 'how' about the deceased. That's not much, is it?" Landis asked.

"It is a start, doctor," Horace told him.

"Shoes are given a name. It is identical to the style you wear, Doctor Balfour," she said.

"They're called a Balmorals Boot," he told her.

"How very interesting. Such an old-fashioned style for a young man."

CHAPTER FIVE

"Haggerty, you say? Charlie Haggerty huh? And just the name in a shoe? That's not much to go on, Never heard of him, so he's probably not from these parts," Chief Garrison moaned, slumped behind his desk. Even with an electric fan blowing air in from the window, the room was hot and stuffy.

"Right now, that is as good as it is going to get. Besides, you'll be investigating it. All we can tell you is that we don't know the cause of death until we get back the lab reports in a day or so," Doctor Landis said as he handed the police chief his report.

"Any idea when it happened?" he asked, looking at the forms.

"Maybe a day or two ago, and it stands to reason it was before he was put in that ferry box. He's well past rigor mortis, but in this weather, to be locked up in a closed box like that, out in the sun, it's hard to say. The confines of the box and this heat, plus the humidity, skews the decomposition rate of a body. Speeds it up. If I made a guess, I'd say within the past few days," Landis told him. "Maybe we'll get lucky with the lab reports, but I wouldn't count on it."

"A couple of days ago is just about when my prime suspect was working before he disappeared, and if he isn't the prime suspect, then the killer got away. Mac had some jibberish about a fellow wanting a job, but never got his name. He's on my list, too, whoever he is. What I can't figure out is how the body got into a box on the chain ferry," the chief said.

"Well, good luck, chief," Doctor Horace said. "We're going to enjoy the rest of the summer and read all about the story in the *Com-*

mercial Record. A life of pampered ease, that's for us, right, Beatrix?" He turned to Doctor Landis and Beatrix, and asked, "Ready to go?" They were.

"You do know that Chief Garrison will soon be asking us to assist him, do you not?" Beatrix asked the moment they stepped out the station door.

"I do," Horace said. "I set him up for it. And before you ask, the answer will be yes," he told her. "That is, if you....?"

Beatrix twitched a smile, her eyebrows arched, "Of course!"

Landis stopped and looked at both of them. "Why? Why do you always want to get involved? The last time you got into this game you got shot, Horace. Haven't you got anything better to do with your time than being a target? Or do you miss the bad old blood and gory days in France?"

"You see, that's the problem. We don't have anything better to do. That is, at least I don't. Now, Beatrix has her airplane and art, but even for her, there are just so many paintings a woman can do while flying upside down..."

"Horace! I do not paint while I fly, and certainly not when I am inverted," she interrupted. "Even if I could do it, it would be far too dangerous a stunt!"

"So you see, it gives us something useful to do in our old age. Keeps the mind working and heart pumping," Horace continued to banter back to Doctor Landis.

"The way you talk, I'd almost say you enjoy it," Landis said, shocked.

Beatrix smiled again and said, "We do, but do not tell anyone. It's our secret." She was still smiling when Landis got in his car, and the two of them were walking home. "That was wicked of me, was it not?" she asked Horace.

"I thought it was well done."

"A young woman came by a few minutes ago, looking for you. I hope it's all right, but I put her in your library. I would have put her in the lounge, but I'm cleaning in there and the floor is still wet. I told her that I didn't know when you might be back, but she said she wanted to wait," Mrs. Garwood said as the two of them stepped onto the deck of the *Aurora*. "She seems very worried about something."

"My name is Balfour, and this is Doctor Howell. We're both physicians. How can we help you?" Horace asked when they came into his library.

"The desk clerk at the Butler Hotel said you might be able to help me," she said quietly as Horace and Beatrix sat down. "He said you two were good ... at things."

"Perhaps you should begin by telling us your name," Beatrix said.

"I'm sorry. It's just that I'm at my wit's end. My name is Sally, ah, Sally, ah, Randall. Sally Randall."

"And why are you at your wit's end?" Horace asked.

"Well, you're probably going to think I'm a terrible person. But I was to meet someone here for the weekend," she said, her eyes down.

"No, not at all. Many people come here for the weekends," Horace said. "I take it that he never arrived. Is that right?"

"Yes," she said, fighting back tears. "I'm worried something has happened to him. See, I came up from Chicago on the *South America*, and he said he was coming by train and would meet me on the boat dock when I got here. He wasn't there, and I haven't seen him since I got here. I don't know where he is!"

"Sometimes travel plans are changed at the last minute. Perhaps he couldn't get away from work, or a family member took ill..." Horace suggested, trying to comfort her. "Or, maybe he missed his train connections." Horace paused, then told her, "Then again, he might have changed his mind."

"What is his name, Miss Randall?" Beatrix asked quietly.

"Charlie. Well, Charles, really, but everyone calls him Charlie. Charlie Haggerty. He's a professional golfer," she said.

Beatrix looked stricken, and barely whispered, "Oh, dear," then looked at Horace as he blew the air out of his cheeks.

"Unfortunately, there is some very bad news," he said quietly, drawing on a lifetime of experience when he had to give the same message to a patient's family. He'd learned to deliver all the news as straight forwardly as possible, gently but without sugar-coating it. It hurt, but it was the kindest method. "As I said, we are both physicians, and you should know we assisted the local doctor with an autopsy..."

"Charlie?" the woman gasped.

Beatrix interrupted. "We believe so. There was no identification on his body, but his name had been stamped in his shoes. There is, of course, the very small chance of a case of mistaken identity, but I do not believe you should get your hopes up. I must tell you his death is highly suspicious. As of right now, we do not know the cause of death, but I am quite certain he did not suffer. I am also quite certain the police chief will want to interview you. If nothing else, he will request you to identify the deceased."

Miss Randal looked at Beatrix, then Horace, and back at Beatrix again. Her eyes were wide and she looked terrified. To their surprise, she jumped up and ran out of the study, across the deck, and down the gangplank. Horace and Beatrix quickly followed after her, but she was soon lost in the crowd on Water Street.

"That was an unusual response," Beatrix observed.

"It certainly was. I don't recall a reaction like that before."

"Something is not right. I believe there is far more to this than we know," Beatrix answered, still scanning the sidewalks. "We must avoid jumping to conclusions."

"I think it may be a bit late for that," he answered quietly.

"What do you mean?"

"To begin with, we're already thinking and talking about this as a murder. Logically, that is what it appears to be - murder. But if we think that way, a murder is all we are going to see. For all we know, the deceased was out on the town, had too much to drink and passed out. Maybe he was with some friends who were also lit up and decided to put him into the box on the ferry. He'd come round and start pounding and shouting until someone let him out. He'd be sore as anything about it, but his friends would have a good laugh.

"Or, maybe he had some sort of seizure, and when his friends realized he was dead they got scared and ditched his body. Or, it could be something else. Thunderation, that puncture wound on the neck could have been a thorn on a rose bush, for all we know right now. All I'm saying is you're right - we can't jump to conclusions, and I think we may have made a few jumps already."

Beatrix said nothing, considering what he had just said. "There is another possibility. What if Mr. Haggerty was married and stepping out on his wife with Miss Randall? Someone found out and killed him. A lover's triangle is yet another possibility," Beatrix added. "It is not unknown for a betrayed wife to get her revenge."

"Yes," Horace said quietly, chagrined that she had even thought of that angle. For a moment he wondered if she had been reading too many movie star magazines with lurid stories of actors and actresses. "Or, perhaps the fellow who cranked the ferry got into a beef with him and did it. Then again, maybe they are married and she is the scorned wife, or he was an inconvenient husband?"

"Speculating will get us nowhere. The important thing is to have an open mind," she told him.

"Yes, and let's hope that Chief Garrison has an open mind when he finds Bob Campbell."

"I find that highly unlikely," Beatrix said with disdain. She turned to Horace and smiled, "In that case, I do hope he is at least smart enough to recruit us!"

Horace laughed. "Trust me, he will, and like we told Landis, we'll agree to it."

"It would be wise on his part to do so. Horace, I do not believe Miss Randal is quite who she wants us to believe she is."

"How so?"

"For one thing, she was wearing her straw boater, but the bow on the band was on the left side."

"That's where I wear mine," Horace interrupted.

"Yes, of course you do. A man's hat bow is on the left side; a woman wears hers on the right. She was perfectly, even flawlessly attired, except for that mistake."

"Yeah, well, maybe she was distraught and in a hurry...." Horace suggested.

"I have reason to doubt it," Beatrix replied. "Furthermore, she hesitated when she gave us her name. Distraught or not, people know their own name, and we cannot assume the name she used was her real one."

"I'll say one thing, you weren't jumping to conclusions when you noticed he was athletic. She just told us he was a professional golfer. And, you found the right name on his shoes," Horace said quietly.

"The second time," Beatrix answered, shuddering at the memory of her mistake. "So, now we wait?"

"So now we wait," Horace stated firmly.

Horace and Beatrix had retreated to a couple of deck chairs to read, when Fred and Phoebe returned. "Good to see you again," Horace waved, hoping Fred would take the hint that all was quiet. "Good shopping trip?" he asked.

"Oh, I'd say the girl bought enough fruit and vegetables to feed the Russian army. When I told her you liked beets, well, that was a mistake. She bought plenty. We have a generous peck of them. And don't you go counting on me to eat them. You ask me, they taste like dirt."

"Why don't you finish carrying all that stuff on board with her, and then see if you can rustle up Theo, and tell him to come and join us. You, too," Horace suggested.

Fred laughed. "They're right behind us, hauling in produce. The minute Doctor and Missus Theo saw you two down to the Chain Ferry, and then heard me and Miss Phoebe were going for a joyride, the two of them said they wanted to go with us. I guess he didn't want any part of your detectivating." He looked over his shoulder at the car. "They're waiting to hear if the All Clear has been sounded before they come aboard."

"I see. Well, give them the high sign and tell my brother we need him, would you?" Horace asked.

For the next few minutes Horace and Beatrix told Fred and Theo about their morning's activities. The two listened attentively, and then Theo leaned back and said, "Not much to go on, if you ask me. A dead body, but there's no certainty it was even a murder, and just too many variables. And that woman, Sally Randall, you said? She seems like an odd one, from what you said. How'd she give you the slip so fast?"

"I mentioned that Chief Garrison would probably want to talk with her and she made a dash for it. I believe the modern phrase is 'took a powder,'" Beatrix said. "I believe I may have frightened her. Or, is it 'on the lam'?"

Horace reached over to touch her arm. "Not your fault," he said, hoping to comfort her. She didn't reply.

"Makes you wonder, don't it?" Fred asked. "No idea where she's staying, I take it."

"We never got that far," Horace answered.

"No, Horace. I believe you are mistaken. She came here on the advice of the desk clerk at the Butler Hotel. We can safely assume that she is staying there."

"I think you ought to let Garrison know," Theo said softly.

"I agree. All he knows right now is the name we found in the deceased's shoe. Even if what we know isn't much, you're right that he ought to know about this woman," Horace said. "Well, Beatrix, want to stretch your legs and hoof it over to see the chief a second time this morning?

"All things considered, I never really want to see that man. No doubt it is essential this time," she said icily.

"Well, before you go, Horace, I need to see you for a moment in private. Your study?" Theo asked.

As Theo closed the door behind him, Horace asked, "A bit early for a bump, isn't it?"

"That's not why I'm here, and you know it. Look, you remember our talk the other day?"

"Yes."

"Well? What have you decided? About you and Beatrix?"

"We've been a bit busy. She had a rough flight back and was exhausted, and this morning, well, you know about that. We've been busy, and now isn't the time," Horace explained.

"No, and my guess is you're happiest having it that way. That's why you're leaping into this case. One of these days you two are going to have to switch off that brain and turn on your heart, or you're both going to end up getting hurt."

"When the time is right," Horace said evenly, masking his rising temper. "Right now, Beatrix and I need to go see the chief."

CHAPTER SIX

Horace and Beatrix had just reached the White House on the corner of Water and Mason Streets when Horace stopped and nodded toward a bench. "Let's give this a bit more thought before we rush ahead of ourselves," he suggested as they sat down. He was not in a good mood after the brief conversation with Theo, and wanted to be sure he was focused on the mysterious death of the late Charlie Haggerty.

"What are you thinking, Horace?" she asked.

"Well, since you're in no rush to see the Chief in the first place, and since we don't have any medical evidence yet, maybe we should have another conversation with our Miss Randall before we see him."

"If she is willing to talk to us," Beatrix cautioned.

"I agree, but I think she might be more willing. She reacted emotionally at the news. By now, she will have had a few minutes to collect herself and might be more willing to talk. I've experienced it many times in the past when I had to give a family bad news. They become emotional, then settle down again. The problem is where to find her? She ran off in this direction. And, I know she said she was sent by the fellow at the Butler, but perhaps that was a ruse. So tell me, Irene, if you were in Saugatuck for a romantic weekend with your beau, where would you want to stay?"

"I have no frame of reference to answer that question. I have never had a beau, and certainly no experience with an illicit liaison," she said, starting to blush.

"Understood. But, the question remains."

Beatrix thought for a few moments and cautiously said, "I would certainly not stay at any of the guest houses. There would be too much conversation and too many probing questions. I would want to stay somewhere larger to be more anonymous." She paused and faintly smiled. "Hide in plain sight. I think our next stop should be the Butler. Let's hope we're right the first time or she might skip town before we do find her."

Horace stood and held out his hand to help her to her feet. This time, to his surprise, she took his hand, then dropped it once she was on her feet.

"Miss Randall?" the desk clerk at the Butler Hotel asked. "Yeah, she's in. She came in a few minutes ago to get the key to her room. Looked to me like she had been crying. You think she is okay?"

"She had some rough news. Doctor Howell and I thought we would check up on her," Horace explained.

"Room two twelve. I haven't seen her come down, so she's probably still there, unless she went down the back stairs." The clerk nodded toward the stairs, indicating they could go to her room. "You want Cal to go up with you?" Before they could answer he tapped the brass gong for the bellhop.

Cal instantly appeared, leaving Horace to explain that they could find their way on their own. He handed him a dime for his efforts.

"Miss Randal? It's Doctors Balfour and Howell. We saw you a few minutes ago on the boat. May we come in?" Beatrix asked after Horace had knocked on the door. They could hear some movement in the room before Miss Randall opened the door. She had a cotton handkerchief in one hand to dry her eyes. She motioned for them to come in the door, then hurriedly locked it behind them. Considering the turn of events, it wasn't surprising that she had pulled closed the drapes.

"You've had quite the shock," Horace said. The woman nodded in agreement, but said nothing.

"And, we were concerned for your well-being," Beatrix added.

"Thank you," Miss Randall whispered quietly. "That is very kind of you."

Horace and Beatrix sat silently, waiting for her to talk first. "I never expected it. I thought perhaps he had changed his mind or something like that. I wouldn't be the first girl to get stood up, now would I? But I never expected he'd end up dead. You don't know how he died, do you?"

"We are not certain. It will be another day or two before we might know, and even that is not a certainty," Beatrix answered. "We can only hope to learn something of his passing."

"As I said earlier, because of the circumstances," Horace said cautiously, "the police chief is treating it as a suspicious death. That is very understandable and routine. And, that truly, I assure you, is all anyone can say. Right now it is suspicious. Nothing more, nothing less. Suspicious. However, because it is all so out of the ordinary, the chief will be doing his own investigation, and he will need to talk with you."

"I understand," she said. "You said identifying the body, whether it really is Charlie or not. Maybe it is someone else. There's always hope." She was trying to be brave.

"There is something else you must understand. You came to us because someone on the staff here told you that we were good at certain things, investigations. And, yes, we are. We are very good. In the past we have worked with the police chief at his request. As of right now, this moment, we are not working for him. Is that clear? Do you understand?" Beatrix asked.

"Yes, I think so," Miss Randall said. "Sort of private eyes, right?"

"You should also know that he may ask us formally for assistance at some time. As of right now, that means you can speak freely with us and it remains confidential. Physicians are not required by law to tell anything about someone they are treating to the authorities," Beatrix carefully explained. "Because of the way you came to us, we can remain quiet, at least for now."

"Which means, if you want to tell us anything that might be useful, then right now, rather than later, is the best time," Horace said firmly. "I know this can't be easy..."

"No, no, it's not. I met Charlie a couple of months ago where I work and he suggested coming to Saugatuck for a weekend. He said he'd been here before, to play golf, I think, and that it was a nice place. Some of my friends have been here, so I thought 'why not?'" Miss Randall said.

"What was his line?" Horace asked.

"Work, you mean? Charlie was a professional golfer. He's the club pro at a place near St. Charles, you know, Saint Charles in Illinois, and he wanted to move on. He's got dreams, you know. He thought he had what it takes to play in the tournaments. Maybe he did, maybe he didn't. But, he had ambition, and that counts for something in my book. A girl likes that in a man. I got my ambitions, too, you know."

"And what do you do?" Beatrix asked.

"I'm a chorus girl at a club on the north side of Chicago," she said. "Someday I'll audition for the headliner spot, and I'll get my break.

When that happens I'll make the most of it, and that's for sure. I got my ambitions, too."

"You are a singer in the chorus?" Beatrix asked.

"Yeah, that too, on some of the numbers," she tried to stifle a smirk. "Mostly me and the other girls dance behind the mainliner." Miss Randall's answer was confusing Beatrix. "Look, I'll be straight with you - it's a vaudeville joint, and one night Charlie came in, and we started talking and sure I know it's against the law, but everyone wants a little fun, and all, so he bought me a couple of drinks. I think the owner pays off the coppers. Charlie was a real gentleman, respectful, and didn't put the moves on me like some men do after they buy a girl a drink, sort of like it's their right or something, if you get my drift. After that we went out a few times. He was sweet, a real gentleman, not like a lot of Stage Door Johnnies."

"Do you know if he had any enemies? Someone who might want to harm him?" Horace asked.

"No," she said flatly.

Beatrix looked away from Sally and asked, "And what about you? Do you have anyone who might wish you harm?"

"No. I mean, there's always some rivalry in the dressing room. Things like that. And, all of the girls want to get noticed and move from the chorus line to being a star. You know, competition, but it's no cat fight, if that's what you mean. We look out for each other. And sure, there's competition for a rich guy. Just that sort of thing," Sally replied. "Nothing serious. I mean, I've seen it at other joints. They're all pretty much the same."

"I see," Beatrix answered. "Might there be a man who was jealous of Charlie?"

Miss Randall thought for a few moments and shook her head.

At the end of a long silence Horace finally asked, "Well, as I said, we're not working with the police as of yet, so if there is anything else you want to tell us, I urge you to do it now."

Sally shook her head. There was nothing she wanted to add.

As Horace and Beatrix stood to leave, he turned to Sally and asked, "By the way, what's the name of the place where you work?"

"The Batavia Club," she answered.

"You wouldn't happen to know the name of the owner, would you?" he asked.

"Sure, I do. Everyone on the Northside knows Mr. George Moran owns the club and a bunch of other speaks," she said almost brightly. "I met him a couple of times. He's a real swell, but kind of creepy. Some girls go for that sort of man, but he's not my type."

"Thank you," Horace said, urging Beatrix out the door. "When you are ready to talk more, you know where to find us. I hope it is soon."

"Well, what do you think, Horace?" Beatrix asked once they were out on the street. "And is this Mr. Moran important?"

"Yeah, he's important, and no mistake about it. He runs the big gang on the north end of Chicago," Horace told her flatly.

"What does that mean?"

"It means that Moran and Al Capone are rivals. Deadly rivals. They've been at war for a few years, ever since O'Banion was killed. Right now, I'd say that our Charlie Haggerty's death was no accident."

Beatrix suddenly shuddered despite the warm sunshine. They walked half a block in silence before Beatrix asked, "Horace, do you think that Miss Randall is what they call a 'gold digger'?"

"Well, if she isn't, she'll do until another one comes along," he muttered in disgust. "Thunderation! Maybe she's just hoping to find love."

"Horace, there is something else that is bothering me. Miss Randall said that she came to see us because the desk clerk told her we were good at certain things. I assume by that, she meant investigations. But what did she really want us to investigate? Did she want us to search for her missing friend? Or, do you think she already knew he was dead?"

Horace stopped short, blocking people on the sidewalk as he turned to face Beatrix. "That, that, is something that had not crossed my mind. Good thinking. That could change everything."

"Yes, perhaps. I do not believe the woman is to be trusted."

.

CHAPTER SEVEN

This time it was Beatrix who said, "We are in no rush. Perhaps we should think this through, and plan what we are going to tell the chief."

"You're right," he said softly.

"Horace, all we know for certain is that Charlie Haggerty is dead under suspicious circumstances. Very likely he *was* murdered, but we cannot discount robbery as a motive since his wallet is missing. You know that I rarely let my emotions get the best of me, but I am on pins and needles waiting for the lab reports. And as for Miss Randall, I question her honesty."

"I agree with you about Haggerty, and I am also very sure, positive, that Campbell is not the killer. His boss Mac said he was a good kid, and already had plans to go into Chicago. That leaves him out, right now, even if Garrison thinks he's a suspect. That other fellow is an uncertain factor. For all we know, Mac killed Haggerty and then came up with the story about this other man wanting a job. He certainly had the opportunity. Now, why do you have doubts about Miss Randall?"

She looked down for a moment, trying to find the right words. It gave Horace just enough time to pull out his pipe and light it while she collected her thoughts. "Horace, this is somewhat embarrassing for me to say to you, but I am not quite as naive as you might think, and I do not want to lose your respect. That is important to me." She paused and finally continued. "Miss Randall said she was a chorus girl. When I asked if that implied she was a songstress, she smirked. I expected that because I believe most of the young women who entertain at an establishment of that nature are, well, to be forward and blunt, floozies! I do not believe they are decently attired when they are on stage, and their dancing is very suggestive, if you understand what I mean."

"I see," Horace said, trying not to smile. "You know, I've heard it said that they were 'fast women,' and it seems like you just confirmed it."

"I believe many of them are of rather casual, perhaps even easy, virtue," she added. "It is not information I wish to know."

"Well, I can't see how knowing that would ever lead me to lose respect for you, Beatrix. Why, if anything, I am grateful you have more knowledge of the world than I," he said gently, still trying hard not to smile.

"In turn, perhaps we will find she is not entirely trustworthy. There is a possibility that she is somehow involved in Mr. Haggerty's death," Beatrix said quietly.

"She set him up?" he asked. "Perhaps killed him, even?"

"We must keep that in mind."

"Then that's all the more reason to see the Chief so he can bring her in for questioning," Horace answered quickly. "The sooner the better!"

Beatrix put her hand on his arm for a second to slow him down. "There is also another possibility we should bear in mind. Perhaps it is exactly as she said. Perhaps they were here in Saugatuck for a romantic liaison and he was murdered and robbed. Or, perhaps there is some other reason...."

Horace interrupted. "What other reason?"

"That is the unanswerable question right now. However, he was not here to play golf. I am positive of that! There are no golf courses," Beatrix said firmly.

"I didn't know that," Horace replied quickly. "That's something. I don't know what it means just yet, but it's something. How do you know there aren't any golf courses here?"

"For the simple reason that I fly, and I've flown over this area many times. If there were a golf course I would have seen it. The nearest is in Holland, and in South Haven in the other direction."

"Yes, of course. So, either Miss Randall is lying or Charlie Haggerty enticed her up here under false pretences. Perhaps, he is not quite who he claimed to be."

"Or, perhaps they were staying in Saugatuck and he intended to play in a nearby area," Beatrix countered.

The two stared into the distance, thinking, until Beatrix asked, "Tell me you have a plan."

"Maybe, but it isn't much of one. We need to go back to the boat and talk to the others."

"I thought we were going to see the Chief," Beatrix objected.

"We are, but Theo and Fred first. We need to put our brains together. And, it's time for Phoebe to start earning her keep. I have an assignment for her. Then we'll see the chief."

"What if Miss Randall bolts in the meantime?" Beatrix asked. Horace didn't answer, and was soon striding down the street with Beatrix hurrying to keep up.

"Sorry, but we need to make this fast, and then go see the chief," Horace explained when he had assembled the others.

"I thought you had already done that," Theo said, his eyebrows shooting up in surprise.

"We were about to do it, but we saw Miss Randall first, and there is some news. And, I, that is, we, need your help," he told them.

For the next few minutes he and Beatrix took turns as they told them about their conversation a few minutes earlier. "Now, the interesting thing is that she told us that Charlie Haggerty had come up to golf, but there are no courses around Saugatuck or Douglas. That means there is either some serious duplicity, or something is greatly amiss."

"So, here's what we want you to do. Fred, go snoop around. The coffee shops, pool hall, anywhere you can think of where you might hear what people are saying. Get the gossip. Anything about Charlie Haggerty or anything else, but primarily having to do with golf. Oh, and go over to the barbershops and talk to the shoeshine boys. See if they polished his shoes a couple of nights ago. And, if you see any of them out on the street, ask them, too."

"Yes, Sir, General!" Fred readily agreed.

"Theo, I'd be grateful if you and Clarice would find out where you can play golf," Horace told his brother.

"But we don't play," Theo objected.

"You know that. I know it. We all know it. But people in town don't know it. Just find out where the nearest courses are. That might be helpful. If you get a positive answer, see if you can find out who can give you some lessons, and then do a little probing."

"All right," Theo agreed, "but I don't think it's going to get us anywhere."

"I know, but humor your big brother, would you? And then turn the conversation a little, and steer them into letting you know if someone is thinking about building a golf course."

Before Theo could object, Horace turned to Phoebe. "Well then, young lady, you want in on this case, so you're on. There is something you can do for us. I would like you to go to the telephone office and see if the operator, Bobbie, as I recall, has a Chicago area directory. Start looking for golf courses, and get the names and numbers for us."

"Names and numbers of Chicago area golf courses. Got it," Phoebe said with a smile. She was included in a real investigation, and it made her feel very grown up. "I'll take a notebook with me and a pencil. Two pencils, just in case the lead breaks on one!"

"I knew we could count on you. All right. Everyone has their assignments. Let's see if we can all meet back here at two-thirty. Meanwhile, Beatrix, time for us to face the music," Horace said triumphantly.

"Horace, I thought we were going to see the Chief, not attend a concert," Beatrix objected.

"We are," Horace answered, once again caught off guard by how she often took him so literally.

"Not so fast, big brother," Theo said firmly, waving Horace and Beatrix to sit down again. "From what you just said, maybe this Charlie Haggerty tried to sweet talk your Sally Randall into coming up here. Flip it and see it from a different angle. What if she did the sweet talking to get him to come up here? Maybe she was the set-up woman. You ever consider that?"

Horace and Beatrix stared blankly at Theo for a few seconds. "No, that would never have crossed my mind," Beatrix answered quietly.

"It's certainly worth keeping in mind," Horace added. "Thunderation! That muddies the water all the more!" He turned to Beatrix and motioned that they should go see Chief Garrison.

The chief was in a good mood. "Well, just like Mac said, the Campbell boy got himself on the train back from Chicago with his friends. I got him in the back room, letting him sweat it out for a while before I grill him."

"I take it the fellows all vouched for him," Horace said.

"Vouched and even had their ticket stubs from Wrigley Field. Campbell even showed me his program and score card. Looks like that part's on the up and up, at least but I still got plenty of questions for him. Maybe he didn't have anything to do with it, or maybe he did. Coming back here might have been a smart move on his part so no one was suspicious. I'll get it out of him one way or the other," the chief boasted.

"We have additional news for you," Beatrix said quietly. "When we came back from the autopsy there was a young woman waiting on Doctor Balfour's boat, by the name of Sally Randall. It appears that she had a relationship with Charlie Haggerty. You will find her on the second floor of the Butler Hotel, in room two-twelve. I suggest you hasten over there before she leaves town."

"You just let her go?" the chief spat out, his cheerfulness instantly gone.

"We had no reason to detain her," Beatrix objected. "And, I am quite certain we are not working as your agents, would you not agree?"

"No reason? She's a witness. She knows something. For all I know, she might have killed this Charlie Haggerty! And you just let her go waltzing off the boat?"

"More like the hundred yard dash," Horace said sheepishly. "She was in my library and when she heard Haggerty was dead she bolted out the door and we couldn't find her on the street."

"Big help, you two!" the chief fumed. "I'd better get over there and haul her in, too. And you'd better hope she's still there. You don't happen to know what her line is, do you?"

"She stated she was a dancer in a chorus line at a club owned by a Mr. Moran. A Mr. George Moran of Chicago, I believe," Beatrix answered. Slowly.

"Moran? George "Bugs" Moran? Bugs Moran! That's just what we need around here."

"Why?" Horace asked.

"Why? I'll tell you why. Bugs Moran and Big Al are enemies, rivals, trying to control the booze and every sort of vice imaginable. You ought to know that. Not just in Chicago, either, but the whole area. You know what that means?" the chief demanded. Before Horace or Beatrix could answer, he answered his own question. "It means that there's a good chance they're going to try to stake out a claim here and we'll have Tommy guns blazing away up and down the streets."

Beatrix was silent, staring straight ahead, her face blank.

'It's not good news, if it comes to that," Horace answered.

The chief was so stunned by his own words that he instantly calmed down, and with a long sigh of resignation barely whispered, "Then I'd better go find this Miss Randall. Room two-twelve, you say?"

Horace just nodded.

They followed the chief out the front door of City Hall and the two of them moved to a bench on the opposite corner. "Something is very wrong, Horace," Beatrix said, putting her hand on his arm. "You are very pale."

"It brought back some old memories," he said flatly. "Painful ones."

"All physicians, surgeons and pathologists, have their private cemeteries of mistakes and patients they couldn't save. Learning from them is one thing; dwelling on them is a maudlin luxury we cannot afford. Right now, we have something we must do. You must regain your composure and focus on this."

Beatrix completely misunderstood Horace's dismay, but rather than explaining it, he remained silently lost in past memories of his son caught in the middle of a gang war.

"Horace, do you realize that we have made no inquiries as to where Mr. Haggerty was staying?"

Her question roused his mind. "You're right! We need to find out."

"I suggest we go across to the Butler and inquire at the desk. If Miss Randall has a room there, it is logical that Mr. Haggerty suggested the hotel, and that means it is very likely that he reserved a room." Beatrix stood up, ready to move on.

"Haggerty? Charles Haggerty. Yes, he checked in, room two-four-teen," the desk clerk told them. "Cal, you took him up, didn't you? The registry book says it was right at one o'clock in the afternoon." Horace asked for the room key and was surprised the clerk handed it over. "Guess it's okay, seeing as how you two are private eyes for the chief. Chief is in the next room if you want him. Say, I heard he's the fellow that was killed, wasn't he?" the clerk whispered. Horace and Beatrix ignored him.

"I suggest we adjourn to the dining room until Chief Garrison comes down and leaves," Beatrix whispered urgently.

"Yes. Good thinking. And, let's hope it is with Miss Randall. Maybe this gets resolved quickly, and without Bugs Moran and Al Capone mixed up in it," he answered. They walked quickly through the lobby and took a table in the middle of the dining room where they could watch the front entrance. Before the waitress could get to their table to take their order the Chief and Miss Randall walked out the front door. Beatrix observed that he was tightly holding her arm, either to steady her or to keep her from running away.

Beatrix abruptly got up from the table and led the way to the stairway going up to the rooms. "Convenient, isn't it? Next door to each other. It looks like they were going to have a romantic weekend, after all. So far, that part of the story holds up," Horace said quietly as he unlocked the door to Haggerty's room.

They stepped in, closing and locking the door behind them. "This is not the type of behavior of which I approve," Beatrix said firmly.

"Breaking into a dead man's room?" Horace asked.

"No, not that. This is of necessity. I mean the behavior which I believe both of them intended to commit while they were here, and without a marriage license."

"Oh, I see," Horace answered, turning to one side so Beatrix would not see the half-smile on his face. "Well, it's obvious that nothing happened here. The room has not been touched. I think he probably came into town, put his grip on the bed and went out. Let's have a look in his bag and see if there are any clues."

For the next few minutes they carefully lifted out each article of clothing, then Horace felt along the liner of the suitcase. "Nothing. Shirts, trousers, socks, underthings. Not so much as a book to read on the train," he said.

"It's what is not here that I find intriguing. We were told the man was a professional golfer and Miss Randall said he was coming here to play golf. He apparently deceived her. There is no bag of clubs and no golfing shoes," Beatrix said quickly. "Then again, perhaps it was Miss Randall deceiving us."

"Unless he took them out to the golf course and left them there," Horace suggested.

"Horace, for a man of your age, you can be dreadfully naive. We aren't in the Victorian Age anymore. Furthermore, as I remember distinctly telling you earlier, there are no golf courses nearby. I suggest we return to your boat and await the others."

"Not just yet. I want to see if this door is unlocked," Horace said, taking the knob on a door on the interior wall. He smiled when it turned.

"What are you proposing?" Beatrix asked.

"As long as we're here, let's take a closer look at Miss Randall's room, shall we?" he asked.

"It is highly unethical," Beatrix said slowly, then quickly added, "but perhaps very helpful if we wish to gain further insight into her, ah, personality. I believe Sherlock Holmes would approve."

He chuckled, "Irene Adler certainly would."

The two quickly looked into the wardrobe and the bureau drawers. "My, Miss Randall must have been anticipating some very warm weather. Her night dress is very lightweight," Beatrix said, then gave Horace a wink to let him know she was teasing.

"I agree. Why else would she bring these two feather fans?" Horace asked, pointing to the open suitcase.

"That is very odd," Beatrix bantered back. "I am beginning to suspect that neither Mr. Haggerty nor Miss Randall had any intention of playing golf."

"I think you are probably right. Look, let's back out of here the way we came and get out of here," Horace suggested.

"Yes, I agree that we should. I would find it discomforting to be snooping in someone's room when they return."

By the time Horace and Beatrix dropped off the key at the front desk and forced themselves to slowly walk out of the hotel and back to the *Aurora* the others had returned and were waiting for them.

"Well, who wants to go first?" Horace asked enthusiastically.

"No real luck with the shoeshine boys, Boss," Fred said. "Maybe they polished his shoes, maybe they didn't. I guess they don't look at faces as much as they do shoes. The boy down to Dominic's said he did a lot of wingtips this week. Not much help. Sorry."

"Well, it was a long shot. Thank you for trying. Phoebs, what about you?" Horace asked.

"Grandfather, there are a lot of golf courses around Chicago!" Phoebe said. "There are so many even I said 'Thunderation!' as I wrote them all down."

"So, how did you manage to get them all?" Clarice asked.

"Well, Bobbie the operator said I could use the Chicago telephone directory, and told me to look in the Yellow Pages for golf. And that's what I did! I wrote down the names, plus the addresses and telephone numbers. That is what you wanted, isn't it? You only said to get the names, but I thought more information would be better."

"Well done! I think you did a better job than even Doctor John Watson! Someone earned herself an ice cream at Parrish's this afternoon. Do you have the list with you?"

Phoebe handed it to her grandfather. He quickly scanned it, thanked her again, and explained he'd go over it much more carefully a bit later.

Theo coughed to clear his throat. "Well, there aren't any golf courses around here. Seems that everyone goes down to South Haven or plays in Holland. And, by the way, our old friend Snarky is a regular duffer in South Haven...."

"That confirms my observation from the air," Beatrix interrupted.

"Good. That resolves that question," Theo replied. "There's more. Now, there is plenty of talk about someone wanting to build a course just west of Douglas, between the road to Ox-Bow and the lake, but so far nothing has come of it. We heard he's waiting for a backer to come through with the money. And guess what name kept coming up?"

"Douglas Fairbanks? Or is it Andrew Mellon?" Horace teased.

"Yeah, right," Theo answered sarcastically. "I'll tell you in one word - Capone. Rumor has it he wants to have a course here, complete with a fancy club house!"

"No," Beatrix moaned.

"Golf course, club house, the works," Theo repeated. "You know what that'll mean? A lot of high rollers from Chicago coming here. Probably a casino and speakeasy. Gambling, booze, all the rackets in one place. The Atlantic City of Lake Michigan. All they need is the boardwalk."

"Well, Chief Garrison was worried about Capone turning up here," he said quietly. "Maybe he was on to something."

"Or in on the deal," Fred added.

CHAPTER EIGHT

As they sat talking on the deck of the *Aurora* Horace happened to glance at Beatrix. She was pale and shaky, and her face was drawn. "Are you all right?" he whispered to her.

"No. I must get out of here." She stood up and walked rapidly to his study and closed the door. Horace was right behind her.

"What's happened?" He asked, quite certain that she was physically ill.

"I must get out of here. Leave!" She clenched her fists and fought back from breaking down in tears. "I want to get in my plane and leave here forever and just go back to Minneapolis. And you should leave, too! Order Captain Garwood to pull up the anchor and go home, and take Harriet and Phoebe with you. We can't be here anymore!"

Horace said nothing, knowing that it had to do with their conversations about Capone and perhaps Moran. Still, he quickly tried to determine if he had said anything that might have set her off, and was sure he had done nothing wrong. Finally, in a bare whisper, he said, "Perhaps you are right. This isn't our fight. It's not even our investigation yet. And maybe you are right about it not being safe here for Harriet and my granddaughter."

Beatrix said nothing, but looked down at the floor, her arms folded tightly over her chest, trembling, not fully realizing that he was agreeing with her..

"Before we can do that, we need to get your plane fixed, am I right?" he asked.

"Yes. Please, would you ask Fred to drive me up to the airfield in Holland. I am sure there is a mechanic who can drive here and fix it. Yes, ask Fred."

"All right. He's still here. I'll ask him to take you up there right now. Would you like me to come along with you? I will, you know."

"I know you would. Sometimes it frightens me that you and I would do anything for each other. But no. Fred can take me up and I'll make arrangements," she said.

"Beatrix, it frightens me, too." He left it at that, not explaining himself. "I'll speak to Fred right now."

Horace and Fred soon returned to the study. "Doctor Howell, the boss tells me you need a lift up to Holland to the airfield. Something about oil getting into your gas tanks. Pardon me for saying so, but I've been taking care of the Balfour cars ever since I got out of the Army. If it's just oil in the tank, that's what I'd call a cake walk. I can do it for you, and it's a whole lot cheaper than hiring some mechanic. Quicker, too."

Beatrix looked at him and answered, "All right." Her voice was flat. "We can go as soon as you are ready."

"Well, now's as good a time as any. Let's get a move on; we're burning daylight," Fred answered.

"Take your time," Horace whispered as his driver and Beatrix left the boat.

"Don't worry, I'll get it fixed and checked and double-checked," Fred said.

"Good. There is no need to hurry back here," Horace added, looking over his glasses to make his point clear.

"Beatrix all right?" Theo asked when Horace rejoined the group.

"She will be. She's a little edgy and claustrophobic when she hasn't got her plane. And listen, before you bring it up again. Beatrix and I talked and we have an understanding, so drop it."

"What sort of understanding?" Theo asked.

"A private one. A very private one." Horace stood up again and went for a walk. He was also jumpy and itchy after being with Beatrix when she was so anxious.

The first, and then the second dinner gong sounded, and Fred and Beatrix had not yet returned. "I have a good idea where they are, but I don't know when they'll be back," Horace explained to Mrs. Garwood.

"Should I hold dinner?" she asked.

"No. They know when dinner is served, and after all the work you've done in the galley, we're not waiting. Perhaps a plate set aside for them, or there are restaurants," he told her.

They had just finished their salads when Fred and Beatrix pulled up and parked the car on the street. Even from that distance, Horace could hear them laughing. "That's a good sign," he said to himself.

"All fixed," Fred said as they came about. "Right as rain and good as new."

"Congratulations. I figured you could fix just about anything," Horace said. "What did you have to do to get it going?"

"Like I told Doc Howell, a little oil in the gas tank is a cake-walk to fix. Truth be told, I've had to do it to your car a few times when you tried being helpful. You remember the time you put oil in the gas?

Good thing you stick to doctoring and leave engines to me. Anyway, I drained out the tank, and then we went up to that aerodrome in Holland and got a couple of cans of gas to bring back, and I done did put it in the tank. That's what took us so long."

"And it took longer than I had expected to get the gas into the carbonator," Beatrix added. "Fred had to throw the propeller just to get a pop out of the engine. It did not start easily with some of the oil still in the engine itself, but now it is running exactly as it should. How did you say it, Fred?"

"Firing on all eight."

"Yes, that is correct. Firing on all eight. Tomorrow I will take it up for a test flight. I will circle the field several times, and if all is sounding as it should, then I will go up to the aerodrome and top off the tanks.

"Fred, if you ever get tired of working for Horace, I will hire you on the spot as my mechanic," Beatrix teased.

"Wonderful news! Now, sit down and have dinner. You two are falling behind," Theo said.

"You will not!" Mrs. Garwood said loudly as she bustled out of the galley. "Not until you go and wash your hands. And from the looks of the two of you a little soap and water on your face, if you please! I'll not have you eating with that muck on your hands, and then getting sick and saying it was my fault. Go! No! Wait right here." She dashed into the galley and returned with a couple of veteran towels that were destined for the rag bag. "I'll not have you getting that filth on my good towels. These will be better."

After dinner Horace invited Beatrix to take a stroll through town. "You seem more relaxed now that you can fly your plane again," he told her.

"I will know for certain tomorrow after the test flight," she answered.

"And, you still think we should up stakes and go home? Or, weigh anchor and sail off, might be more like it?" Horace asked. "Both, I guess."

"No, perhaps not. I found it very confining earlier today. The mention of Capone and this George Moran and their machine guns... his nickname is 'Bugs.' Why is that?"

"Because he is buggy. It's slang from the war. Someone who was acting very strangely was considered to be 'buggy'. Moran is very buggy and unpredictable. That's what makes buggy.

"As I was saying, I found it confining not to be able to escape if it was necessary. I am much calmer now," she said.

He was grateful, but quietly reminded her, "we can always leave if it gets too intense."

The two of them strolled down Butler Street and climbed the stairs to get to the hill. "We'll wander a bit and circle back," he suggested.

Beatrix didn't say anything.

"You know, I'm getting rather fond of Saugatuck. Remember when we were growing up in a town much bigger than this one? he asked.

"I do. Saugatuck is quite similar," she agreed, smiling at the thought of the few happy moments of her childhood. They walked on in silence, watching three boys play keep-away by kicking a can on the street, and in the next block two young girls were jumping rope. Almost every front porch was occupied by one or more people, and all of them waving or saying 'Good evening' to them as they walked past.

"Well, there you are," Beatrix said, nodding toward a For Sale sign in front of a large brick house. "You like Saugatuck so much, maybe you'll want to move here."

Horace didn't know if she was teasing or not. Even if he had not dared talk about it out loud, even to himself, he had thought more and more about moving to the village, maybe helping the town doctor if he got busy or wanted to go fishing. It seemed like a nice place to spend his latter years. But then he would push the idea away and out of his mind. Too complicated, too many changes, and he'd probably miss the little portion of his old medical practice the Young Turks had left to him.

Their quiet stroll was interrupted when Doctor Landis pulled up next to them. "I drove over to see you, but your sister-in-law said you were out for a walk. Place is small enough I knew I'd find you before long," he said out the window.

"And why were you looking for us?" Horace asked.

"On account of the fact that I got a call from the laboratory, and there is no sign of poison or anything else in his system. Not a thing. So, that makes that puncture in his neck a real mystery, doesn't it?"

"It sure does," Horace admitted.

Beatrix interrupted. "Doctor Landis, I assume you have the body in the mortuary?"

"Yes, why?"

"And cold?"

"Got him on ice. Standard procedure until the chief releases the body, and then we got to find a funeral home and the next of kin."

Her eyes widened in excitement. "I know the hour is late, but location of the puncture has stayed on my mind. I was hoping it was poison because that would be an immediate answer, but now that we know it is not I think I know. This is an imposition but I think we must have another look. If I am right, I doubt it will take very long." She turned to Horace. "Theo is the better of you two in neuro-surgery, isn't he?"

"Yes, definitely," Horace answered without hesitation.

"Doctor Landis, will you drive us back to the boat so we can get Theo, and then to the hospital? It is important!"

"Well, yeah, I guess so. Sure, why not? Hop in. Say, I forgot. I have another passenger in the back seat. A young lady who said someone special owed her an ice cream."

"Are we going for ice cream, Grandfather," she asked.

"I don't think so. Not tonight. It looks like we have some work to do, I'm sorry."

"Well, can I come with you and help. Maybe I could be your secretary or something," Phoebe offered.

Almost in unison all three doctors answered, "No!"

"I'll tell you what. We'll go twice tomorrow," Horace said.

They pulled up to the *Aurora* to let her off. "Phoebs, see if your uncle Theo is there, and if he is, send him down right away. Tell him 'STAT' - he'll know what that means."

"STAT?" she asked.

"Yes, so hurry."

A few minutes later Theo bustled down the gangplank. "Well, fill me in," he asked.

"I got the report back from the labs, and there is no poison. More accurately, no detectable poison. Doctor Howell wants to examine the body again," Doctor Landis explained.

"And that's the emergency? Couldn't it wait until morning?"

"No, Theo, it cannot," Beatrix explained calmly. "When we first examined the body I thought the puncture wound was in an unusual location. Now, I have a very good idea what happened."

"I think you mentioned something about an embolism," Landis said.

"This could have waited until morning, you know," Theo snipped.

"No, Theo, I do not believe so. Time is of the essence. And, should my suspicion be confirmed, it means that Chief Garrison can release Bob Campbell from custody," she explained. "And, Doctor Landis, as soon we get to the hospital, perhaps we should call Chief Garrison and invite him to be present."

"Why?" Horace asked.

"Because if I am right, it would be to everyone's benefit if he sees it. Otherwise, I believe, he will not believe it."

"Agreed," Landis said. "Seeing is believing."

They mutually decided that Theo would do the surgery, with Horace assisting, while Beatrix supervised. "And I want to be in the gallery to see this. I've stayed away from anything this exotic," Landis had said. "This is big league stuff."

"Good. There is no reason why we can't open now, and then we will be ready for Garrison," Beatrix said. She nodded at Theo to begin exposing the carotid artery. "I know you are experienced with this, but please do not nick it." The work was slow and methodical: Theo lengthening the incision, Horace exposing it.

"Chief, you are just in time," Beatrix said, then explained what they had done so far.

"Good," the chief said uneasily.

"I doubt you can see anything from across the room. Please step closer," she told him. "Please put on a mask. It is for your own protection." She waited for him to put it on.

"Now, as you can see, we have exposed the length of the artery from the incision up to the brain. It is the carotid artery. Doctor Theo is now going to carefully open it for us. Proceed, please."

They all watched intently as he worked. "It would help if you told me what we're looking for," Theo said.

"Yes, that is my fault. We are looking for an embolism that blocks the artery. Slowly, please. If it is there we may see it very soon......"

They all watched in silence. "Stop! There it is! That is what killed him!" Beatrix said in triumph. She took the scalpel from Theo to use as a pointer. "Right there. A blood clot. Mr. Haggerty died almost instantly from what is commonly called a stroke." She was almost giddy with excitement.

"So, it was natural causes! He died of a stroke," the chief said. "Case closed."

Beatrix glared at him, and very slowly said. "Far from it. This clot was created when someone, someone who knew what they were doing, used a syringe to inject air into his artery. It would not have been an accident, but pre-meditated murder."

"Lady, I've never known you to have much of a sense of humor, but you've got to be pulling my leg. A bit of air killing someone? You're batty. We breathe that stuff all the time and it hasn't killed us. Tell her doctors: She's batty," the chief complained.

"I'd hear her out if you want to solve this case," Horace said firmly.

"You ever see this before, Doctor Howell?" Doctor Landis asked.

"Just once. This is the second time. A syringe of air, injected into an artery will cause a blood clot. Whether it is a heart attack or a stroke, it will cause death," she said firmly.

"Air like you and I are breathing right now?" the chief asked.

"Yes. Pure oxygen will not. It will be absorbed into the body almost instantly. But air is sixty per cent nitrogen. The nitrogen forms a bubble and travels toward the brain, in this case, until the artery is sufficiently narrow to cause a blockage. When that happens the patient strokes out. If they are fortunate, it is instantaneous death. Otherwise, it can lead to permanent paralysis or a neurological vegetative state. As tragic as it is, in one sense Mr. Haggerty was fortunate."

The news staggered the chief, and he sat down hard on a stool. "Definitely murder," he mumbled.

"Definitely murder," Horace, Theo, and Horace all repeated.

"This is something that Bob Campbell could not have done. It takes someone who understands sufficient medicine to know where to inject the needle," Beatrix said.

"Yeah, so maybe he didn't do it. But what about that woman, Sally Randall?" the chief asked.

"It is highly unlikely," Theo said. "Whoever did this had to be strong enough to hold Haggerty, and tall enough to do it. She misses out on both counts by a country mile. I think the time has come to release young Mr. Campbell."

"Yeah, you might be right. But I don't want him leaving town, and that's the only way I'll let him go. He's got to agree to that or he stays put."

"Look, I'll finish up here and suture his neck. It's journeyman's work and won't take long. You three go along with the Chief and spring young Bob," Landis offered.

"I sure can't thank you enough for getting me out of there. I didn't have anything to do with killing someone. And Mother's been worried out of her mind," Bob said, shaking hands, twice, all around once Horace, Theo, and Beatrix were standing outside the jail.

"How about stretching your legs and breathing some clean air, then? We'll walk you home," Horace proposed.

"You two go right ahead and do that. I shot off the boat so fast I didn't tell Clarice where I was going. By now she'll be getting a bit lonely for me. And, what a story to tell her!" Theo said. "Beatrix, that was a good solid piece of diagnosis."

When Mrs. Haggerty saw her son, she wrapped her arms around his neck to kiss him, and then sobbed against his chest. "I can't thank you two enough for what you've done for Bob," she said through sniffles.

"Well, we had a good idea that he was innocent. It just took a little show-and-tell to convince the Chief," Horace said. "And I'm sure what Bob would like right now is something to eat. I have my doubts the Chief is any good in the kitchen."

"That's for sure!" Bob laughed. "Say, thank you again. I owe you - big time for all you did."

"Tell you what, a free ride on the Chain Ferry will be plenty," Horace said. "Well, it's getting late, and I'll bet you two have plenty to talk about."

Beatrix rattled Horace when she put her hand on his arm as they walked back to the *Aurora*. "You surprise me sometimes, Horace. You do truly have a heart. We did the right thing seeing Bob Campbell home. You are a good man. Always remember that."

CHAPTER NINE

"Congratulations, again, Beatrix," Theo said the next morning over breakfast. "I credit your experience and observation for that one."

"Thank you," she said quietly.

Then turning to both Horace and Beatrix, Theo added, "You know we haven't solved anything yet, don't you? You identified the cause of death, not the killer."

"Yeah, I know," Horace sighed. "But we got Bob Campbell sprung from jail and returned home to a very happy mother. That's something."

"And, I think it is highly unlikely that Miss Randall killed him. She is at least two inches shorter that Charlie Haggerty, so it would be almost impossible to have reached up to inject the oxygen. However, if he was sitting and she came up behind him, then it would be possible. I have my doubts that a chorus girl would have the training or the experience to do something like that," Beatrix added.

"If her story is true," Horace cautioned.

"As I was saying," Theo shrugged in resignation. "That leaves just the mystery fellow who wanted a job on the ferry, and quit before he began."

Phoebe who had been absently listening to the conversation as she read another Sherlock Holmes short story, suddenly looked up and said, "But it just can't be him!"

"Why not? Do you know something you haven't told us?" Horace asked quickly.

"No, Grandfather. It doesn't make any sense if Charlie Haggerty was killed at least a day before this man wanted a job on the chain ferry, that's all," she answered. "Or the day he was killed, or the day after. It would have to be the day before the murder."

The three adults looked at her in stunned silence, and it scared her. "Did I say something wrong?"

"No, no, not at all," Theo said.

"I believe Phoebe is correct. It would make no sense for the killer to do that. If he was, oh Horace, what is the slang I am looking for?" Beatrix asked.

"Casing the joint," Horace smiled.

"Yes, that's the term I wanted. If he was casing the joint, why would he spend time, alone, riding with Mac back and forth on the ferry? That would be fool hardy of him, needlessly taking such a risk. This murder was meticulously done in such a way they would not have expected the coroner to notice the method. The two are complete opposites. It could not have been that man, but someone else."

Horace winced in frustration. "The good news is that we have not taken a step backward. We just haven't moved forward."

Beatrix was looking off into the distance, thinking. "Horace, walk with me to the park," she said suddenly as she stood up, walking down the sidewalk at a fast pace before finding a bench and sitting down.

"There is something very wrong with all of this," she said without looking at him. "I keep thinking about when we broke into Charlie Haggerty's room and snooped. We both realized that there were no golf clubs. There were many other things that should have been there. Perhaps the clubs were in the porter's closet for safe-keeping. That would make sense if they were expensive clubs.

"But there were no golf shoes, no tees, balls, or anything else. Horace, do you realize there was no literature about golf? You and I, and every physician we know always brings along at least one medical journal to read. I bring along several so I can stay up to date. It always stops people from wanting to engage in chit-chat with me. Surely, he would have had something to read, if only to give a list of upcoming tournaments, or something at the club where he supposedly worked."

Horace carefully thought through what she had said. "So, you're about to question whether his telling Miss Randal that he is a golfer is complete fiction."

"I believe it is a hypothesis worthy of our consideration," she answered. "I believe we also must take into consideration that even though Miss Randall told us that Mr. Haggerty was travelling to Saugatuck by train, she might be either mistaken or less than honest."

"What do you mean?" Horace asked.

"There are several possibilities. He might well have arrived by train, or driven an automobile up here. Perhaps he was a passenger if he came by automobile. There is even the possibility he might have come on one of the steamships that arrived a day or so before Miss Randal. And, Horace," she added quietly. "With considerable care and perhaps a disguise, on the same boat."

"That's a bit far-fetched, don't you think?" Horace asked.

"Perhaps, and it may be immaterial. As you said thirty-two minutes ago, we know almost nothing except for the cause of death," Beatrix reminded him.

"I see your point," Horace said as he reached for his pipe. He realized Beatrix was looking far off in the distance and had become quiet. "Please tell me you have a plan."

She turned toward him and gave a faint smile. "I do. We are fairly close to the chain ferry, and I believe it would be helpful if you would talk with Bob Campbell. Perhaps he has had sufficient time to clear his brain a little and can remember something that might be helpful."

"All right. And you?" he asked.

Horace was not surprised when she did not answer, but got up and walked toward the center of the village.

"Doc, I can't thank you and your missus enough for getting me out of jail," Bob Campbell said, pumping Doctor Horace's hand as they stood on the ferry landing. "I knew I didn't have anything to do with that fellow getting killed, but the Chief wasn't having any of it, and he's known me since I was young. I sure can't thank you enough."

"I'm glad it all worked out. And when you see Doctor Howell, you might want to thank her, too. She did the heavy lifting on solving how Haggerty was killed and getting you out of there and back home. Bet your mother was happy, too?"

"Say, she sure was. She said she wants to have you and your wife over for dinner. I'd be real proud if you would come."

"We'll talk about it later. And, you might want to keep in mind that Doctor Howell and I aren't married, just medical colleagues. We've been friends since childhood."

"Yes, Sir," Bob said, "Got it right up here," he added, pointing to his brain.

"I need your help figuring out this business. Now, we know you didn't do the murder, and we now know how it was done. The who and why parts are still the mystery, so I came over here. Maybe you remember something that might be helpful."

"I'll do my best, Doc!" he said.

"Well, from what I heard, the last passenger of the night was a fellow with a big car. What do you remember about the car? Let's start there."

"It was a big car. My father, he's dead now, used to call them a doctor's car. Some of the other fellows do, too."

"All right. I know it was just about dark, but do you recall the color?"

"Yeah, that's an easy one. Brown. It was a big brown car with port-holes up in front, right near the engine. Only a Buick is like that," Bob said. "I saw that when we landed. There's a street light right near the dock."

"Now, that's helpful. A brown Buick. You probably didn't look at the license plate or remember the number, do you?" Horace asked.

"Well, when I knelt down to put the chocks under the front tires, and then got up and walked over to the crank, I saw the front plate. I don't remember the number, but it was from Illinois. Does that help, even if I don't remember the number?"

"Right now, that is a big help. More than you know. Now, you're certain there was only one passenger?" Horace asked.

"I only saw one, if that's what you mean. I don't think there was anyone else, but I didn't look too closely in the car. See, when it's a car or truck they don't have to pay per passenger. Sometimes they don't know that and to save money they'll scooch down between the seats. But it was just the one man I saw. He and I talked while we were coming across back into town. Say, if you want me to do it, you could get some mesmerist to put me under. I hear that's a good way to remember stuff you forgot. I don't like that sort of thing, but I owe you plenty, Doc. You and Doctor Howell," he said, pointing his finger up to his brain. "I'd do it for you, if it helps."

"Well, we'll hold on to that idea for later. You've given me plenty to go on for right now," Doctor Horace told him. "And, it looks to me like you got some passengers waiting for you on the other side."

"Yeah, looks that way," Bob agreed. "Say, you want to ride over and back with me? It's on the house, and I'll let you turn the crank if you like."

Horace paused for a moment, and then agreed. He had nothing better to do, and he realized he might learn something useful about the ferry.

When they returned to the landing, Horace had a slight smile on his face. He filled his pipe and walked slowly back to the *Aurora* thinking over what he would be able to tell Beatrix and Theo when they all got together again.

"Fred, Phoebe," Horace began once he had found the two of them. "I have something I'd like you to do. Now, this will sound like a fool's errand, but maybe it will turn something in our favor."

Phoebe slid to the edge of her chair, suddenly remembering her "Paris Manners" and sat up straight. She was eager for the assignment. "We'll do it, won't we Fred?" she asked with excitement.

"Very simply, I want you to drive around town," Horace said. Then, remembering that he had been giving Phoebe driving lessons, he added. "That is, Fred you drive, and Phoebe, you're going to be the scout. I want you to look for a big brown car, probably a Buick, and with Illinois license plates. Saugatuck and Douglas, both of them, and out along the beach road and to Ox-Bow. While you're at it, you might go through the cemetery once or twice, too."

Phoebe carefully wrote the instructions in her notebook. "Brown car, maybe a Buick, and with Illinois plates, right?"

"That's right," her grandfather said.

"And what if we do find this brown Buick with Illinois license plates needle in a haystack?" Fred asked.

"Phoebe, you keep scanning the streets as you drive. You, too, Fred. If you see anything that is brown, slow down. And if is the right car - the brown Buick, then get the license plate number. That's important. That's the important part."

"And then pull over and grill them?" Fred asked.

"That, Fred, is the one thing I don't want you to do! You understand? Just drive slowly like you're trying to find a parking place. Get the license number and get back here. Don't rouse their suspicions, is that clear?"

"You mean like spies?"

"Phoebs, that's the ticket. Spies," Horace said. "And Fred, if you're being followed, then you drop Phoebe off in front of a store. Phoebe, you go into the store and you stay there. Fred, you get back here and we'll pick Phoebe up as quickly as we can."

"Once the coast is clear, right?" Fred asked.

"Once the coast is clear. All right, you two; you got your assignment. Good luck and good hunting," Horace said. "Now, Phoebe, here's a dollar. If you have to go into a store, buy something and make sure they put it in a paper bag for you. That way it'll look like you are shopping."

"Haven't heard you say that since we were in France, General," Fred smiled, stood up, and saluted. "You remember the time we were low on supplies and you sent me and a couple of ...."

"Another time, Fred," Horace told him.

"And is this important, Fred?" Phoebe whispered as they went down the gangplank to the car, confused at their assignment.

"Might be, but it's important to your grandfather, and that's what counts. We're spies, so keep your eyes open."

Beatrix had been gone for a little over two hours when Horace spotted her striding rapidly in his direction. It instantly quelled his anxiety about her well-being. If she had at least told him where she was going, it would have given him some comfort.

CHAPTER TEN

Beatrix had walked directly to the police chief's office in hopes of speaking with Miss Randall. "I released her from jail and put her under house arrest at the Butler Hotel. You'll find her there. At least she'd better be there!" he told her.

"Chief, may I ask why you chose to do this? It seems out of the ordinary," Beatrix said.

"Two reasons. I didn't see any reason why the village should have to pay for her food, and it costs money to keep someone locked up. So, I marched her back there and told the manager she was staying put. She could sit in the lounge, have her meals in the restaurant or stay in her room. Makes no never-mind to me. She just can't leave the hotel.

"And second, I wasn't getting anywhere with her. You can lean pretty hard on a man who gets arrested, but it doesn't seem right doing it with a woman. No decent way to soften them up and grill them until they confess.

"That answer your questions?" the chief demanded.

"Yes, thank you. You may have been extremely wise. That is why I would like to go talk with her again. Perhaps after some time in your cells she will be more willing to talk," Beatrix said.

"I'll go along with you," he told her.

"Chief, as much as I might appreciate your knowledge of the law and police methods, do you not think she might be more willing to open up if it were just woman to woman?" Beatrix asked, forcing a smile.

"Have at it. Just make sure that if she gives you anything, you let me know."

"Of course, Chief," Beatrix answered, still focusing on holding a smile.

"What do you want?" Miss Randall snarled at Beatrix. "Did that cop send you over to get something out of me, because you're wasting your time."

Beatrix swallowed and said, "No, you are mistaken. I stopped by the jail to see how you were doing, and the Chief said you were back at the hotel. I came here because I know this has been a difficult time for you."

"Geez, I'm sorry. I shouldn't have been so rough on you. Sometimes a girl doesn't know who she can trust."

"Miss Randall, as a physician, I understand. There is no need for an apology. So, may I come in for a few minutes?"

"Sure, make yourself at home. And, yeah, it's been rough. I mean Charlie getting killed and all, and then the Chief thinking maybe I did it. And now stuck here. I'll bet the club fired me by now since I was supposed to be back a day ago."

"Yes, it has been hard," Beatrix said, waiting for her to respond.

When the woman said nothing, Beatrix said, "Miss Randall, I am perhaps old enough to be your mother, perhaps even your grandmother, but I am neither a prude nor naive. I say that because when Doctor Balfour and I saw you I noticed a couple of large feathered fan in your open suitcase. Doctor Balfour may have thought they were angel wings for a costume party. You and I know better, do we not? I believe you may be what is called a 'fan dancer' who works in a nightclub. Am I correct?"

Miss Randall let out a long sigh of despondency. "Yeah, guilty as charged."

"It is quite the art form, and takes considerable dexterity. So, just as you had secrets about your professional life, perhaps there are more secrets about Mr. Haggerty or your relationship with him. Do you know for certain that he was a golf club professional?" Beatrix asked.

"Maybe....I honestly don't know. If it was a line he was using, well, at least it was different from barbers trying to pass themselves off as bankers. Charlie said he was, and he looked athletic, that's for sure. But I never saw him with no clubs or playing, if that's what you mean."

"But if you had your doubts, why did you walk out with him?" Beatrix asked.

"Now you're showing your age, Doc. Walk out? That sort of dates you. Look, he was good looking and he was always a gentleman. You think a girl finds that sort of a man in the places I've worked? They buy you a drink and think you can pay them back from neck to knees, if you get my meaning. He wasn't that way. Not at all. Charlie was a real gentleman, and dressed like he was the Arrow Shirt man. So what if he fibbed about golf? He was a decent guy and he had plenty of money."

"What do you mean when you say plenty of money?" Beatrix asked.

"Well, it's not like he had no big roll of C-notes or something. And he didn't flash it around. The thing was, he always paid for everything with a brand new twenty dollar bill and then put the change in his pocket. He did it all the time. I just figured he'd take the small stuff back to the bank and get some more new twenties."

"That is unusual. Most people detest breaking a bill like that, and when they do, they spend the change until the next time they must do it," Beatrix said distantly.

"Maybe it was just his way of letting people know he had money. Like I just told you, he never talked about it or flashed it around. Some men do that to make an impression, but they're usually phonies.

"Look, if a decent enough guy wants to take me out and buy me dinner and show me a good time, why should I spend my money on grub? I'm saving my dough cause I don't want to work in speaks the rest of my life. I'm socking my money away to get me started in Hollywood, so if a man wants to pay for dinner, I'll let him."

"As a strictly economic plan, it seems well considered. How do you think the owner of your club will feel if you leave?"

"Him? He's going to be plenty sore. That's why I gotta get back or he'll think I took a powder and scrammed. One of the girls tried that and he slapped her around pretty good when she came back."

Beatrix gasped at the thought of violence, then slowly let out her breath. "Miss Randal, you have been very, very helpful. I know you do not like being forced to stay here, but we both know it is better than in the jail. And I want you to listen very carefully to what I am about to say and think about it. I believe from what you told me, you are far safer here than anywhere else right now."

"Yeah, maybe. I get jumpy being cooped up like this," she said. "You want to come by, do it. I'll be nicer the next time you knock."

Beatrix stood up. "Thank you."

Beatrix walked slowly down the main staircase and was about to go out the front door. She paused and went to the front desk. "Is there a back door?" she asked the bellhop. He pointed her to a hall-way and told her to follow it all the way to the back.

She knew she should stop by the police station, but she needed to walk a couple of blocks to think. A stroll through four blocks later, when she stepped into his office, a clerk told her he was out on a call. "You can wait, if you want," the woman said. Beatrix declined and hurried back to the boat.

Horace was on the deck, leaning on the rail, scanning the street. He spotted her and waved.

CHAPTER ELEVEN

"Beatrix, welcome back aboard!" Horace called as she walked up the gangplank. "You've had adventures, I take it. Come into the study and tell me all about them."

Beatrix insisted on Horace first telling her what he had found out from Bob Campbell. He gave her a brief summary and then said, "I suspect it won't do us any good, but I've got Fred and Phoebe out scouting for a big brown Buick touring car with Illinois license plates."

"Brown?" She shivered slightly. "I have always found there was something troubling about a brown car. It is certainly not logical of me to think that way, but I do. I am never quite certain that the motorist is either capable or completely trustworthy," she told him.

"Now, back to you. What did you learn?" Horace asked.

Beatrix had far more information, and repeated again Miss Randall's tale of how Charlie Haggerty always broke a twenty dollar bill and never used his change. "I think it is quite strange, do you not?" she asked.

"Perhaps. Most of us do things others thing a bit odd." He paused for a few seconds realizing that most people probably thought he and Beatrix were also very odd. "But nothing about golf? Now, that just makes things a bit more interesting. I wonder what sort of work Haggerty was really doing?" His voice trailed off as he tried conjuring up an answer.

Horace pulled out his pipe, filled and lit it, and they sat in silence. Twice, Beatrix reached over to take it from him and have a puff. "Horace, it appears to me that the Butler Hotel will soon be wanting to rent Mr. Haggerty's room.."

"Yeah, you're probably right about that."

"What is your thought about us going over there and offering to collect everything and bring it back here? We would tell them it is for safe-keeping."

"The last thing we need around here is more inventory cluttering things up," he answered.

"I understand that. But it is not merely to hold his personal effects for the next of kin. If we bring it here we can much more carefully examine everything. Perhaps we will find something useful, a clue or two. Furthermore, it will keep his things out of the hands of Chief Garrison," Beatrix explained. "Well," she slyly smiled, "until we have looked at them first."

Horace looked at Beatrix and smiled. "That is sound thinking. And we never did check at the front desk to see if he put his golf clubs in the bell captain's room, either. Good thinking, Beatrix. Let's act like a caisson and get rolling."

"I am not at all certain I understand the metaphor. I was never in the Army, and you were not in the Field Artillery so why would we want to act like a caisson?" she asked.

"Over hill, over dale, something, something, something, the caissons go rolling along. Never mind. Let's go."

The desk clerk checked with the manager who checked with the owner, who came out, and was more than happy to let Horace and Beatrix take everything from the room. He handed over the key and offered the assistance of a bellboy. "I believe we are capable on our own," Beatrix said firmly. The ever dutiful Cal the bellboy trailed behind them in case he was needed, or if there might be an extra tip on a quiet afternoon.

It took them only a few minutes to make certain the bedside table drawers were empty except for a Bible, and then take the suitcase from the wardrobe. "Cal, there is so little here I'll carry it. But, a little something for your trouble," Horace said, handing him a quarter to send him on his way. Once Cal was gone Horace started softly singing, "Pack up your troubles in your old kit bag," until Beatrix told him it was distracting, and he stopped. While he folded the shirt that was on a hanger, Beatrix looked under the bed. "Nothing," she reported. "Now, help me lift up the mattress."

"Good idea. A perfect hiding place," Horace agreed. Standing on one side of the bed, they lifted it up. Their efforts were rewarded when they saw a large thick envelop between the springs and the mattress. "And what do we have here?" Horace asked.

"I think you will find out only after you open it," Beatrix told him. "I believe it would be much safer if we waited until we returned to your study and locked the door behind us." Horace agreed, especially since the contents felt like they might be cash.

They did not rush to leave the room and calmed themselves walking down the corridor and the steps. "Here is the key," Horace said as he handed it over to the clerk. "By the way, do us a favor and look to see if he left anything in the reception closet, would you? Oh, and the hotel safe, too."

He clerk came out and reported. "A bag full of golf clubs has Mr. Haggerty's name on them. They're kinda heavy; you sure you want to take them with you. I could have the jitney driver haul 'em over to you if you want."

"Thank you, but we will take them," Beatrix said firmly. "I will carry the suitcase. Doctor Balfour, will you take the golf bag? And please, no more war songs."

"There is a thin possibility we may be tailed," Horace told Beatrix as they walked down the front steps. He saw her shudder, remembering the frightening experience a few weeks before when they were investigating the death of Fairy Nightshade. "I hope not," he added as a bit of cold comfort.

"We should put the suitcase and clubs in your study and then come out on deck for a while," Beatrix advised. "If we were followed, they will be less suspicious if they see us on deck. Perhaps there is some coffee or lemonade in the galley."

"You just shattered the old adage about women being curious," Horace teased.

"Perhaps. But another adage is that it was curiosity that killed the cat. We must give the appearance of restraining our interest."

"Lemonade, it is," Horace said as he returned with two glasses. They sipped at their drinks slowly as they leaned against the rail, looking at the people and scene below. "Looks like everything is all right. Let's go look at the suitcase," he told her.

"And who truly is the curious one now?" she teased. "Which one shall we inspect first, the suitcase or the golf bag?"

They started with the golf bag, removing each club one by one, inspecting it before moving on to the next. They moved on to the large holder for the clubs. "I can't feel anything out of the ordinary," Horace said when he withdrew his arm from it. He picked up the bag, turned it upside down and shook it. "Nothing." Together they inspected the bottom and were disappointed.

"What about these pouches?" Beatrix asked.

Together, they laid out an assortment of golf balls, tees, and a few cloths for cleaning clubs and shoes. "Not too exciting," Horace said in disappointment. They were finally rewarded when Horace felt something odd inside a zippered pouch. "Like there is something hidden in the lining," he told her.

"What is it?"

"I don't know. It's certainly not solid. I can feel it bend a little.

"At last!" Beatrix said cheerfully.

"I think we're making progress. There is a little loose piece of fabric, tucked in like an envelope. Yes, here we go. I am carefully pulling apart the envelope along the inside wall of the pouch....and I am inside. I have it. It feels like paper, and if I am correct...." He paused until he had extracted the contents. "...and it looks like cash because it is cash."

"Horace, this takes us back to a month ago. I hope we are not contending with another blackmailer," Beatrix said.

It was an assortment of small bills: ones, twos, fives, and tens. Beatrix began laying it out by denomination while Horace continued to probe the recesses of the golf bag for more. He found a second and then a third cache, all of small bills.

"What do you think this means?" Beatrix asked, looking back and forth between the money and Horace.

"Right now, I haven't any idea. It could be something innocent, such as where he kept his cash out of sight instead of flashing it around. Or, perhaps he was wagering on golf tournaments. That would explain why he brought his clubs to Saugatuck even if there isn't a course anywhere close. I think we ought to look at the envelope we found under the bed," he told her.

He lifted the suitcase onto his desk and opened it, then the envelope. Horace pulled out a thick pile of twenty dollar bills, and let out a whistle. He handed her about half of it, and they began counting out well over two thousand dollars. Horace looked at the two stacks, then at Beatrix. "That is a considerable amount." Beatrix scooped it up and returned it to the envelope.

"Interesting," Beatrix said. "I certainly approve. Mr. Haggerty was obviously a very methodical man given the way he has divided up his money. It leaves me curious as to what he might have been carrying on his person when he was waylaid."

"Yes," Horace said slowly, thinking. Somehow, there was more to it than a man being methodical about how he carried his money. "That's an awful lot of money for anyone to carry, Beatrix. I'm not speculating just yet, but it's odd."

"You are right, of course," she said, then smiled. "We must not get ahead of ourselves. And the real question is what do we do with all this money? Do we take it to the police chief now or later?"

"I think later would be better. We'll have Fred tuck it away somewhere for safe-keeping."

"You realize it is the second time this summer a murder seems to revolve around money, do you not?" she asked.

"I do. Fairy Nightshade was a black-mailer. I wonder what Mr. Haggerty's story might be."

"Good question." Horace held one of the two dollar bills up to the light to see if there were any unusual markings on it. He didn't find anything. "Maybe you'll have better luck with the microscope," he suggested.

"Perhaps I should do the work. Go away somewhere for a while and leave me to work in peace. I become claustrophobic with someone hanging over my shoulder and watching me," Beatrix said. She looked at Horace in dismay. "Please forgive me. I did not mean to be rude."

"You weren't, and there is nothing to forgive. You have your methods, just as I have my way of doing things." He went to the book shelves and selected a mystery by Dorothy L Sayres, then added, "Phoebe's idea. I'll be on the deck when you are done."

Horace had only turned a couple of pages before Phoebe and Fred returned. "Any news?" he asked. Before Fred could answer Phoebe winked at her grandfather and said, "Well, we didn't see anything the first time we drove through town, so I suggested to Fred that maybe we should go to the cemetery and look there, just in case they were hiding out. Well, they weren't there of course, but Grandfather, I asked Fred if he would show me how to drive, and he did, and then he let me take a turn...."

"Boss, your granddaughter is a natural at it. She put it into gear, knew just how to use the gas and clutch better than most drivers I've seen. Your girl is no gear-jammer, and that's for sure! Why, if I give her a few lessons, I'll bet she could be the first female Barnie Oldfield," Fred interrupted. "She's natural at it behind the wheel." He turned to Phoebe and asked, "You sure your ma hasn't been teaching you how to drive?"

"No, Fred. Mother hasn't taught me how to drive, I promise," she said solemnly, then winked again at her grandfather.

"Thunderation! If you don't mind, you were sent out to scout around for a brown Buick touring car from Illinois. Did you find one and see who drives it?" Horace asked.

"Well, kinda-sorta yes and no, which is to say we saw a Buick matching that description, but we didn't see who was in it. It's parked over on Lucy Street further down the river," Fred told him. "Now, my guess is that it's been sitting there a while on account of it being all dusty."

"Grandfather," Phoebe interrupted. "Maybe it's hot!"

"Well, if it's sitting out in the sun, with this sun, it probably is hot," Horace answered, teasing her just slightly.

"No Grandfather, 'hot' can also mean that it's stolen," the girl told him.

"I see. Now that is useful information. Right now Doctor Howell is doing some research in my study, but when she is done, I want you to tell her what you discovered. And thunderation, you two, don't say anything about driving lessons. Your mother will be angry enough with me as it is. Now, I mean it. Not a peep!"

"Yes, sirree, Boss. I got the same message from Miss Phoebe. Don't you worry - not a peep."

"Now, is there anything else besides you two skylarking around?" Horace asked.

"There might be. It's a definite maybe, and on account of that fact I don't want to get into it any too quick. I need to scout around, and I'd prefer to do it on my own," Fred said quietly.

"That's not exactly helpful, Fred," Horace cautioned him.

"I know that. Now, this might be a genuine wild goose chase, and then again maybe it isn't. You gotta trust me for a little while longer, and I'll come back and tell you which way it is."

"Thunderation! You just stuck me in the waiting room! This had better be worth it, that's all I have to say. All right, go on, but find something good. And Fred, watch your back," Horace said.

"You can count on that, General."

CHAPTER TWELVE

"I just saw Fred going down the street like an ambulance chaser looking for a new client. Any idea what he's up to this time?" Theo asked when he and Clarice returned.

"For all I know, that's exactly what he is doing," Horace said with a tinge of resignation in his voice. "He's off on some scouting mission. You? What did you two learn?"

"Maybe something, maybe not. And you and Beatrix? Learn anything useful?" Horace asked.

"I think we did. We just don't know what it might mean. It's beginning to sound like we have a lot of *maybes* around here. The one thing I know for certain is that Mrs. Garwood said we're having a lot of vegetables for dinner tonight and the rest of the week - thanks to Fred, you two and Phoebs buying out half the crops around here."

"Oh, don't worry about that. We left plenty for the others," Theo teased. He looked at the street next to the boat. "And right now, my guess is you've got more to worry about than what we're having for dinner. That's Harriet's rattle-trap. Looks to me like she's got up a full head of steam."

"Thunderation! I need to make myself scarce and scram."

"Little late for that now. She's already spotted you. What'd you do to upset her this time?" Theo chuckled at his anxious brother.

"I'll tell you later if she doesn't tell you about it right now." Horace turned toward his daughter-in- law as she stepped aboard.

"Clarice, Horace, Theo! I need your help. Our last figure model quit on us. We were already short two, and now we're down to none. Please tell me you can find someone. Even one would help. We don't pay much, but they get free room and board. Start looking! I'm desperate, and I've got to get back to Ox-Bow right now to deal with another matter."

"You want us to find a young lady who will take off all her clothes and stand in front of a bunch of strangers while they paint a picture of her?" Theo asked.

"Not stand; pose. Figure models pose! Yes, that is exactly what I want!" Harriet shot back.

"That's a little beyond our usual line of work, Harriet," Theo said slowly.

"You two are detectives. Go snoop around and find someone!"

She turned to leave, got half-way down the gangplank and turned around. "Oh, and how is Phoebe? Is she behaving herself and staying out of trouble?"

"Definitely. Absolutely," a very relieved Horace told her. The brothers watched her leave.

"All right, spill the beans, what had you worried?" Theo asked.

'Oh, nothing really. Just that Fred gave Phoebe a driving lesson out to the cemetery. I figured she might have gotten wind of it or something. That's all."

"Right," Theo answered sarcastically, "and I'm the Kaiser's uncle. I know you well enough. You've been giving her driving lessons, too, I'll bet."

"Any idea where we find a model for Harriet?" Horace asked, desperate to change the topic.

"Not my department, and I wouldn't know about such things. And I'll bet Clarice would like to keep it that way, wouldn't you, dear? Say, what about ....? No, I guess not. Where is Beatrix, anyway."

"In my study doing some research and I don't think we ought to interrupt her. I'd say we're both in the waiting room. And if you're smart, you're not going to tell her about the job opening. Is that clear?" Horace sighed. "Maybe Phoebs would like some ice cream. You two want to come along?"

"Not this close to dinner. I don't want to kill my appetite. Not with all those beans and beets and tomatoes waiting for us. And that goes for your granddaughter, too."

"Let's forget the tomatoes. Full of nightshade, and last year sort of put me off the stuff."

Harriet returned in time for dinner, still frazzled. "I had to get away from Ox-Bow," she explained. "The staff and our backers want to operate it like a business, and the students come up here and want to work on their art and then have a good time. The creatives and the business people don't see eye to eye, and I'm caught in the middle of it. Well, it's both. It has to be creative and a business or it will fold. And now on top of it, we haven't got enough figure models. But that's only this week. No telling what tomorrow, next week, the weeks after that, will bring!" She looked close to tears, then settled down once she got her frustration out of her system.

"Tell you what. We've got some business to do, things to talk over in my study, so how about if I give Phoebs some money to pay her for her help, and she treats everyone to ice cream?" Horace suggested. "With a bit of luck we'll be finished by the time you get back."

"Well, looks like we've all got news," Horace said when he, Fred, Theo, and Beatrix were in his study. "Fred and Theo, we picked up Charlie Haggerty's personal effects to bring back here, and we found a large amount of cash. Beatrix, please tell us what you have learned so far."

"As Horace said, we found several thousand dollars in cash, nothing bigger than a twenty dollar bill. I have been trying to see if there is a pattern or something of interest for us. So far, nothing. No markings on the bills, everything about them looks like they are genuine, but I must tell you that I have not yet looked at anything larger than a ten dollar bill. I want to finish them first."

"There is still the stash of twenties," Horace explained, interrupting her.

"Nothing so far," Beatrix repeated it. "And perhaps there is nothing. If you do not object, Horace, I will resume my work first thing tomorrow morning.

"By all means, fine," Horace said with a wave of his hand. He turned to his brother. "Your turn. You were trying to find out anything about golf."

"There isn't all that much. We wandered over to the Green Parrot. They've got good pie there, by the way. I did find out that there is a big tournament in Traverse City this week. Several of the top professionals are playing in something they call a Pro-Am Open. I think that means professionals and amateurs are playing, but don't ask me more than that. What I did know is that two of them are Walter Hagen and Gene Sarazen.

"Now, the other thing I heard is that a couple of the business owners and the cashier at the Fruit Growers Bank have taken the train up there in hopes of meeting them. Some of the town boosters want to try opening up a course, and they figured talking with those two players might be helpful. There might be something to it, or it could just be idle talk."

"Excuse me for interrupting," Beatrix said. "I met Mr. Hagen last winter. He had a subdural cyst on his right calf that was bothering him and was at the university hospital. Doctor Walter Belker did the surgery and I did the pathology report. The good news is that a needle biopsy indicated it was merely a benign, non-cancerous fatty cyst, but Doctor Belker wanted me to confirm it. It was Doctor Belker's opinion that it should be excised, but when Mr. Hagen learned it would mean minor surgery, he objected. I believe the decision was made to lance it and drain it. A day or so later Mr. Sarazen and a mutual friend, a Robert Jones, came to visit him. They are all very respectable gentlemen. To have their support and endorsement for a golf course would be a tremendous asset to the aspirations of the boosters."

"Thank you. We'll keep that in mind," Horace said, frustrated at how she had diverted the investigation with her story.

"Fred, you're the real mystery man of the moment. You and Phoebe spotted a brown Buick and then you went rushing off. What did you find out?" Horace asked.

"Well, like Doc Horace said, we went out looking for a brown Buick touring car with Illinois plates on it, and sure enough we spotted it. And while we were out I thought I spotted someone," Fred began.

"Does this have anything to do with the murder? Horace asked sharply. He half expected Fred to have found an old buddy from the war.

"That's the part I don't know. The fellow I spotted looked an awful lot like Brad "the Hammer" Morgan."

"And who is that?" Theo asked.

"Well, it's like this. You see there are a couple of rival gangs down to Chicago, and one of them was run by an Irishman named O'Banion. O'Banion ran his mob out of a flower shop up on the north end of the city and he got himself killed. I hear tell the rest of the mobs gave him a swell funeral - lots of flowers, seeing as that was his official line. After they got him planted six feet down, Moran took over the operation. Well, one of his right hand men was a fellow named Nails Norton. I met Norton in the war when he took a German slug. He plugged the German who done did it, but just wounded him, on purpose like. And then he wouldn't let anyone get him to the rear, and waited until a couple more Huns came to get the wounded fellow, you see, so he could plug them.

"He ended up working for O'Banion. You ever hear the phrase, 'take him for a ride'? Well, Nails Norton was the mug who first said it. Now, like I was telling you, O'Banion was killed and you would have thought that's how Nails would get it sooner and later. Only it didn't happen that way. Instead, he got thrown from a horse and the horse kicked him in the head. Nails got, well nailed. Horse shoe nails, if you get the joke.

"Now here's the thing, this Hammer Morgan was in on everything with Nails Norton like two peas in a pod. The word got out that Hammer and Nails were a couple of thugs to keep shy of, and it was this Hammer Morgan I thought I spotted on the street walking with some other fellow!"

"Thunderation! What in the world is the point to that story!" Horace demanded.

"Just this. Charlie Haggerty was going with that hootchie-kootchie dancer in one of Moran's speaks, and Doctor Howell just told us about all that money he was carrying. And I spotted Hammer Norton up here, all at the same time. It sorta-kinda adds up, leastwise in my head. And then you tell us, Doctor Theo, about these big-time golfers up to Traverse City and some of the business men trying to put together a deal. It really starts to add up fast. Tell you the truth, if it isn't Bugs Moran trying to set up a golf course, then maybe it's the Hammer, but there's still something fishy about the whole thing. Makes a man wonder if Moran sent him up for a look-see.

The four of them sat in silence, trying to determine if Fred had worked something out or not. "Maybe Haggerty ran off with Moran's girl. Maybe she was Morgan's girl."

"And just to keep us all busy, before I forget, Harriet still needs a new figure model," Horace added.

"Horace, that was not being help...." Beatrix stopped in mid word and stood up. "Gentlemen, excuse me please. I must find Harriet." They watched as she jumped to her feet and hurried out of the study.

When she returned, Beatrix said, "Fred, you may have saved Miss Randall's life. I just made arrangements with Harriet for Miss Randall to move to Ox-Bow. We will be driving in Harriet's car to the hotel. Gentlemen, I want you to leave now in Horace's car to get into position. If Miss Randall agrees to the plan, we will be exiting the hotel from the rear. Have your car there, facing out, lights off, engine off. We will come down the back stairs, get into Harriet's car, and drive to Ox-Bow. You are to follow. And gentlemen, I suggest you arm yourselves. Shall we begin?"

"The Chief isn't going to like this," Horace cautioned.

"It is far better to ask forgiveness than ask permission, and in this case, far safer," Beatrix said. "One more thing. When we get to Ox-Bow, I would like you to park at the bottom of the driveway, off to the side. Wait and watch for half an hour before you drive up to the school."

When the three men got in Horace's car, Theo quipped. "Horace, you ever wear a dress?"

"Of course not!" he barked. "Thunderation!"

"Well, it just occurred to me that if you two get together, Beatrix is sure going to be wearing pants."

"That is not amusing! Stay focused, would you?"

"What makes you think Miss Randall will agree to being a model?" Harriet asked as they drove to the hotel.

"From what I understand of her, she is quite accustomed to being very immodestly dressed on stage," Beatrix said.

"How immodestly dressed?"

"Very much so, but with some strategically placed feather fans which she is able to move around to music."

"Beatrix," she gasped in horror.

"Yes, I believe she will be quite comfortable as a model."

"I'm sure she will," replied a stunned Harriet. She wasn't certain whether she was more surprised that Beatrix had found her a model, or even knew where to start looking.

Fifteen minutes later the two women tiptoed down the back stairs and got into Harriet's car. It had given Theo time to start having second thoughts. "I have a feeling we're rushing into something," he said a couple of times. "We should have thought this through a lot more."

"I know, but I trust the way Beatrix's mind works." He leaned up behind the driver's seat. "Fred, Let's go. Keep close, but hold back so we don't draw too much attention."

"Ah, boss, I was sort of hoping you'd have said 'follow that car' like they do in the movies," Fred answered. "And doctors, keep your eyes open for anyone trying to sneak up on us from our flanks or the rear."

They followed Beatrix's instructions, waiting at the bottom of the long gravel trail into the school, all three men out of the car, their right hands inside their jacket pockets gripping their pistols. Even though no one had followed behind them, they were anxiously watching and listening.

"Listen, fellows. I'm going to slip over to the other side and hide behind the trees in case we get some company. And make sure you've got your safetys on," Fred whispered. "I got shot at enough by the Huns, and I don't need to do it again."

"How long have we been here?" Horace asked impatiently.

"Seven minutes," his brother told him. Theo was rewarded with a hissed "Thunderation."

Twenty minutes later they heard a whip-poor-will behind them. "That's not good. There aren't whip- poor-wills this far north," Theo said. All three tightened the grip on their pistols, waiting and listening carefully. "Someone's coming," Horace whispered, listening to the bird song again.

"I would be grateful if you would not shoot," Beatrix said as she came closer. "We can now return to the boat."

On the drive back Beatrix explained that Harriet had found a room in the Old Inn for Miss Randall, adding that she is now using the name Inga Hanson to mask her identity. "Harriet is going to spend the night at Ox-Bow, and asked if Phoebe could stay on the boat with us. She was quite certain her daughter would enjoy it, and that you would not deny her the pleasure of your company. I took the liberty of agreeing with her.

"I believe all will be well. However, we do have a bit of talking to do with Chief Garrison."

"Just out of curiosity, Beatrix, how did you and Harriet come up with name Inga Hanson?" Theo asked.

"Miss Hanson was the Norwegian immigrant girl who worked for your mother when we were in primary school. I am quite surprised you did not remember that. She made delicious pastries," Beatrix explained.

"The pastry part I remember," Theo answered.

CHAPTER THIRTEEN

"Where did Beatrix go this time?" Theo asked when he, Fred, and Horace were sitting in the study.

"When I said I needed to tell Phoebs that her mum was staying at Ox-Bow for the night and she'd stay here, Beatrix said she'd do it in case Phoebe had any questions. So, she's probably getting her off to bed in one of the cabins," Horace answered.

"I see," Theo answered, wincing, and his eyebrows elevated. "Telling her a bedtime story or singing her to sleep, too, I suppose."

"Shouldn't take her too long. She'll join us in no time," Horace said.

"Just one more wrinkle in this convoluted mess," Theo said in disgust. "Dead golfer, a showgirl, and a couple of Moran's boys. What a combination."

To the brother's surprise, Fred was strangely quiet, thinking. "After a while I figure I ought to go out for a walk and see if that Hammer Morgan is anywheres to be seen. Maybe find where he likes to hang out. Probably it'll be the Big Pavilion. And, I'd sure like to spot him and then know he wasn't going up the line at Ox-Bow to outflank them," he finally said.

"Good idea," Horace said. "You mind sitting tight until Beatrix gets here? You want some lemonade? Mrs. G probably has some in the ice box. I'm sure Theo and Beatrix won't say 'no' to something a little stronger, will you Theo?" He slowly filled his pipe.

When Beatrix came into the study to join Fred and the Balfours, she smiled and said, "Phoebe is down for the night. I see I am falling behind. I will not say 'no' to joining you. Horace, a light one, please." He poured her a drink, and they lifted their glasses.

"It seems to me," Theo said, "that if the cashier from the bank went up to Traverse City to talk with those golfers about building a club here, that must mean the president has approved of it. I can't imagine him doing it on his own."

"Only if he was up to no good, so I think you're probably right," Beatrix answered.

"So, hear me out," Theo continued. "If the president knows about it, then he's probably interested. Maybe he sees some profit in it for the bank, or for all I know maybe himself. I think I could go over to the bank in the morning and see if he'd put a long distance telephone call through to his man."

"Go on," Horace encouraged him.

"Well, maybe those golfers would like to come down here and look around and meet some people. Now, if you don't mind putting them up for a night or two, we can get an idea whether or not they're legitimate. If we don't press them too hard, they'll show their hand. And if that doesn't work, we can casually mention a couple of Moran's boys have been hanging around town, and hear what they say to that."

"That might be enlightening," Beatrix said.

"Well, it's just a general idea, and we got all the details to work out. But, if we're going to try getting them down here, then we need to get things into motion or we'll lose our chance," Theo added.

"I see your line of thinking, and I'm willing to have those fellows bunk down here, but do you think this is going to get us anywhere?" Horace asked.

"Right now, I don't know. It's just an idea I've been turning over in my head the last little while," Theo said.

"Well, there isn't much to lose, and we can get rid of some of those vegetables you bought. But, let's sleep on it," Horace suggested. He looked at Beatrix, but she had that thousand-yard stare, and he knew she was thinking.

It was still twilight when they left the study. "Off on patrol, General," Fred said, smiling in anticipation of some excitement.

"I appreciate you doing it. Don't hesitate to wake me if there is something I should know," Horace told him.

"You can count on that, Sir, especially since you got Miss Phoebe here and her mother's out to Ox-Bow. I was just cogitating on it in my mind, and if you don't object, first thing in the morning I thought I'd drive out there and make sure it's all quiet on the front line. They don't have the telephone out there, you know."

Horace put his hand on Fred's shoulder. "Thank you. You're aces, you know."

"One more thing, General, if you don't mind me saying it. You might want to keep your pistol handy in case they try slipping up on us. They might have figured out what we did with that there Miss Randall and come over here to play rough."

Horace looked stricken at the thought. "You might be right. We'll keep watch."

The next morning Beatrix found Horace and Phoebe sitting on the deck, both of them reading. "Good morning. Are the others not up yet?" she asked.

"Well, Fred's out doing some sight-seeing. My guess is he'll drive out to Ox-Bow and see if there is anything your mother needs," Horace said, fibbing just slightly so as to not alarm his granddaughter. "Theo just left to step over to the bank, and I haven't seen Clarice. Otherwise, it's 'hail, hail, the gang's all here.'"

"I see. I would like to ask a favor of you, Horace," Beatrix said firmly. "When Fred returns, would you object if he took me out to the airfield? I really must fly up to the aerodrome in Holland to put fuel in my plane."

"No, of course. Beatrix, you're not thinking of flying somewhere, are you?" Horace asked, a tinge of anxiety in his voice.

"No. But I find it very discomforting not to have sufficient fuel. It is unsettling to have the tanks less than half full," she said quietly, her eyes down.

"I understand. And you'll have Fred there if he needs to tinker with the engine," Horace said.

"You are not jealous, are you?" she asked.

"Absolutely not. Fred knows what he is doing. I wouldn't be much help."

"You are quite sure you are not uncomfortable with this?"

Horace was about to tell her that if she kept asking the question he *would* become jealous, but thought better of it. "I'll come along and see you off. How about that for a plan."

"Yes, it would be much more circumspect that way. I must find some coffee." She saw a thin trail of smoke from the pipe he had put on the table, picked it up and enjoyed a couple of puffs. "Better. Now I will find some coffee." She was smiling.

Horace shook his head. Beatrix was a study in complex contrasts. One moment she was coming to the aid of a chorus girl who wore only a couple of feather fans on stage, and then she gets worried about riding in a car with Fred. It didn't make sense.

"She likes you, Grandfather," Phoebe said without looking up.

"And just how do you know that, young lady?"

"Oh, woman's intuition. Anyway, she told me so last night. I asked her if she liked you, and she said she did."

"I see. And what do you think?" he asked her gently.

"Well, Mother said that Doctor Howell is an acquired taste, but she seems to make you happy, so I'm trying to acquire it, or her, or taste, or *something!*"

"I see. Let's leave it at that, shall we? Say, you want to come along when we go out to her plane?"

"No thank you. Henry from my class is going to the library this morning. He's really smart and, well, some day he is going to become a famous writer!"

"I'll tell you what you just told me, he seems to make you happy. That's what counts. So, I wouldn't keep a future famous writer waiting too long, if I were you. Off you go!" He snorted, "Looks like Fred is back, so we're on our way, too."

"And you're very sure the engine was running smoothly?" Horace asked Fred when they watched Beatrix lift off from the field and gain attitude.

"Yes, Boss," Fred sighed. It was the fourth time he had asked the question in as many minutes. "Now, if he was married to her, he wouldn't be quite so worried," he thought to himself. "And soon as we hear her plane coming back, we'll drive out there, and that's a promise. I figure it'll take her half an hour to get there and land, at least as long to fill the tanks, and half an hour back."

"Thunderation! I'm in the waiting room. Listen, why don't we drive up there, just in case?"

"In case of what? Doc Howell knows what she's doing, and a woman like that doesn't need someone checking up on her every minute. So, yes, Boss, I'd say you're sitting put in the waiting room until she gets back. Besides, any time your brother is going to be back from the bank."

Horace growled.

"Besides, on account of the fact that you're cooling your heals, I can fill you in on all the goings-on at the art camp," Fred answered back.

"Well, start talking," Horace said, leaning up from the back seat to hear his driver.

"Not all that much to tell you. I saw Harriet, ah, Mrs. Walters, that is and she said that it was all quiet last night. Nobody came or went, least wise, not by car. And, she got that Miss Randall bedded down in one of the rooms up on the second floor. I got there just in time for breakfast and that's when Mrs. Walters introduce her new model, and it wasn't long after that, they all went off to paint and draw and such stuff."

"Anything else?"

"Well, kinda-sorta. I hung around for a little while, just to make sure everything was all right, which is kinda-sorta hard to tell at a place like that. I'll tell you one thing, and you better not be telling it to Mrs. Balfour or Doc Howell, but I got a peek at Miss Randal in the all-together, and 'tween you and me...."

"That will do, Fred," Horace said firmly.

"Well, I talked with the bank president and I got some good news. His cashier is staying at a new hotel in Traverse City called the Park Place, and so are those two golfers. And the president is all in favor of the deal. He's got some investors from Chicago who are thinking about putting up the money. So, when I suggested inviting Hagen and Sarazen to come down here to look things over, he said it seemed like a good idea," Theo said as he carried a cup of coffee from the galley to the deck.

"He put a long-distance call through right away, and told his man to convince the other two to take the train down here. He said he'd talk to them and see if they can do it, so it looks like you've got some more guests staying with you." Theo was smiling. "So far, so good."

"I'm still not certain that this is going to get us anywhere," Horace said softly, looking at his watch yet again. "I guess we'll have to wait and see."

"Meanwhile, looks like you've got company, and I'm going to find somewhere to hide out," Theo said, nodding toward the street where Chief Garrison was getting out of his car. Even from a distance, Theo could tell he was not in a cheerful mood.

"You better have some idea where Miss Randall has gotten to," the chief snarled.

"Welcome aboard. There's coffee in the galley if you would like a cup," Horace said.

"If I want coffee I've got perfectly good coffee back to the office," he snapped. "I didn't come for chit-chat. Miss Randall's missing. You got any ideas about that?"

Horace pointed to a nearby chair, then pulled out his pipe to slowly fill it. "You know, you made a right smart decision moving her out of your jail. At first I thought you were just being, well, cheap, doing it. But then when Fred told me he'd spotted a nasty piece of work and his pal here in town, I realized why you moved her."

"Nasty piece of work? What do you mean?" the chief asked.

"Oh, just a couple of Bugs Moran's boys. They're both tough street thugs. I figure the way you keep a close eye on things around here that you must have seen them before Fred did, and you didn't want to say anything. And, don't worry; your secret is safe with us. . You know, I doubt most people realize how dangerous your work can be and how you have to think a step or two ahead of them...." Horace paused to let the compliment sink in. He stalled further as he lit his pipe.

"Yeah, you're right about that. There's more skulduggery that goes on around here than anyone knows. My job is to keep folks safe," the chief said proudly.

"Which explains why you got Miss Randall out of your jail. I wouldn't put it past those two to come in the front door of the station to shoot her, shoot the place up, and maybe plug you. Locked in a cell like that she'd be an easy target. And they're the type who would plug any witnesses too. Thank you for saving us all from a lot of gunplay and bloodshed."

"Yeah, well, I didn't want to let everyone know what I was doing," the chief said.

"And that's why we moved her someplace safe," Horace explained. "Don't worry, she can't leave and make a run for it."

"Well, you should have told me what you were doing!" the chief retorted.

"No, not at all. That's where we disagree. Look, you kept her out of sight, but those two thugs would have found out sooner or later just where she was. Someone, maybe someone at the hotel, maybe a guest, might have said something, and then we'd be back to square one, only this time there'd be a shooting at the hotel."

"Yeah, I see your point, but say, you should have told me just the same!"

Horace took a puff on his pipe and then leaned closer to the chief. Almost whispering he said, "Chief, folks around here need you to keep the peace. We didn't tell you because we don't want you to know. As long as you're in the dark, then you're a bit safer. If you knew, they'd probably beat it out of you, and once you told them, put a bullet into you. This way, if you don't know anything, you're worth more to them alive than dead." Horace leaned back to let the chief think.

"Yeah, I get your drift. But it doesn't quite seem right, not knowing."

"I understand. Truth be told, I'd say the same thing if I was wearing your shoes, but we did it in part for your safety so you could keep everyone else safe. Now, I wouldn't presume to tell you what to do, but I know if it were me, I'd keep someone with me all the time....."

"You mean a body-guard?" the chief asked.

"Yes. A body-guard who is good with a gun in case it comes to that," Horace told him.

The chief leaned back in his chair to think. "Say, I like the way you think. I'd never have looked at it that way. I think I owe you an apology. Here I was thinking you'd gone behind my back, and all the while you were thinking ahead."

"Well, you work to keep things safe around here, and we want, well, I guess, we need to keep you safe as possible. Meanwhile, I guess you're busy trying to figure out Haggerty's next of kin so you can release the body."

The chief suddenly stood up, his right hand out-stretched. "Say, I got a lot of work that's gotta get done. I sure am grateful to you folks. Sure am grateful. Good thing you're on the right side of the law, or I guess we'd all be in trouble."

"Don't forget the idea of having someone with you - your personal bodyguard, so to speak," Horace said gravely.

"Yeah, I sure will."

"And he believed you?" Beatrix asked when she settled into the back seat of the car a little after noon to drive back from the airfield.

Fred couldn't wait to interrupt and answer first. "He did, Doctor Howell. I was there and heard the whole thing. He bit down and took it hook, line, and sinker. I'll tell you, Doc Horace would make a fine confidence man if he ever put his mind to it. And if you don't mind me asking, how'd your plane do, seeing as how I did some work on it?"

"Fred, it ran as smoothly as anything. I had absolutely no difficulty. Not a single cough from the engine. Thank you."

As always, Beatrix was relaxed and exhilarated after she had spent some time in her plane. "Horace, I do not approve of such blatant fabrications, but I must admit it was sheer brilliance on your part. Well done! Now, has Theo heard back from the bank about the invitation to the golfers?"

"Maybe we'll know something when we get back."

For a few moments Beatrix relaxed in the back seat, contently smiling. To Horace's confusion, she suddenly sat bolt upright. "When we return, I need to look at Mr. Haggerty's stash of money. There is something very important I forgot to check."

CHAPTER FOURTEEN

Beatrix had a horrified look on her face, and covered it with her hands as she slumped over the desk in Horace's study. "I have been a complete fool. What an amateur mistake, and it is my own fault because I rushed and was distracted by our experience with Fairy Nightshade's codes," she moaned.

"What is it?" Horace asked.

"Look at the twenty dollar bills. You see it, do you not? It is right in front of us and so obvious I missed it. The serial numbers are identical!" She spread the money across the desk. "All of the numbers are the same."

"Counterfeit," Fred and Horace said in unison.

"Counterfeit," Theo echoed.

"Counterfeit," Beatrix said firmly. "Phoebe would have seen it within a couple of minutes. I missed it. I am so very sorry."

"So Haggerty was a paperhanger," Fred said. "That beats all, doesn't it?

"We don't know that he made his living installing wall paper," Beatrix said.

"A paperhanger is what they call someone who passes counterfeit money," Horace explained. Beatrix didn't respond.

"Outside of missing that detail, I don't think it changes much of anything yet," Theo said. "We still have an unsolved murder, maybe a couple of Moran's men in town, Miss Randall, and possible mob money to build a golf course. What more could we want? And now, we've got one more clue, maybe a major one, that helps explain a few things."

"There's a bit more to think about, and that's for sure," Fred said.

"If Haggerty was passing phony money, then there's a good chance some of that is going to be getting passed around town. And come to think of it, we don't know if that's all of it, or if he was the only one up to no good," Fred answered. He reached for his wallet and quickly checked the twenty dollar bills, then sighed in relief.

"Fred is right," Beatrix answered. "Now, what do we do?"

"It is a police matter, and I think the sooner we tell Chief Garrison, the better. We'll tell him we were investigating Haggerty's personal effects and found it, and that Beatrix saw that the numbers were all the same. I don't see where anything else would be the right thing to do," Horace said. The other three agree.

"What about telling the bank president?" Theo asked.

"Police first. If he wants us to tell the president, we'll remind him it is his job. But, we need to push him to get cracking because if Haggerty spent a lot of it in town, then everyone who has some is going to get hurt," Horace said firmly.

"Horace, do you remember me telling you that Miss Randall said he would always pay with a new twenty dollar bill? I think we know why," Beatrix said. "We thought it was odd. If only we had followed up on it."

"No point in worrying about that. We're doing it now. Fred, gather up all the twenties and put them back into that envelope and bring it along.

Fred chortled and said, "I can't wait to see his face when we show him the money." He unbuttoned his shirt and slid the envelop inside, then put on a jacket. "Better safe than sorry."

"I shudder at the thought," Beatrix said distantly.

"You'd better see this," Horace said when the chief unlocked the door from the inside of his office.

"One of my officers is out having lunch. After what you said, I ....." he sputtered.

"Very good thinking. It's good you're being cautious," Horace said as he put the money on the desk. "Take a look at the numbers, and you'll see why you need to stay on your toes."

The chief looked up and stated the obvious. "They're all the same serial numbers! They're counterfeit!"

"They are. That's what we thought, too. When we went through Haggerty's things we found them and brought them right over to you. It's not our place to tell you what to do, but you might want to tell the bank president about it, and then warn all the merchants and guest houses about it," Theo added.

"And the hotels and restaurants," Theo added.

"You three had better come along with me," the chief said, scooping up the money. "Let's go!"

Outside of an armed robber, few things excite an otherwise staid and solemn banker more than bad checks and counterfeit bills. The president was truly alarmed, almost frantic. "We have to send a telegram to the Treasury Department! No, first thing is to close the bank and have the tellers check their trays. Of all the times for the cashier to be away when I need him here! He froze and looked up at them, "And a couple of high powered golfers coming here to talk about building a course. They'll be scared and take off before anything else happens. And the bank could be ruined! Do you think this is all of it?"

"Take a deep breath," Beatrix said. "Try to relax so you can think. It is bad news, but panic will not be helpful."

"I think you're right about first closing the bank early and looking over all of the money," Theo added. "As soon as you have locked up and told the tellers, then you can send a telegram to Washington. Or better, make a long-distance call and talk to someone."

"I agree," Horace said. "You've got business to do, so I think we should stay out of your way. Chief, you know where to find us." Turning to the banker he asked, "Any word from your cashier on the golfers coming down."

The man's face froze in horror, and he nodded. "Yup, they'll be here day after tomorrow. Just what we don't need right now on top of all of this. You've got to entertain them! I'm counting on you to help us out here."

They left the bank to walk back to the boat, the President locking the door behind them, rattling it to make certain it was locked, and pulling down the shades. "I don't envy them with all the work they've got to do," Horace said. "Not just the teller trays, but everything in the vault has to be checked."

Beatrix added, "I pity the individuals who have been defrauded. And to think only a few days ago we felt sorry for Charlie Haggerty."

"No one deserves to get murdered," Theo said softly, "even for passing phony bills."

"Yes, you are quite right. But the harm this man has done. Those people being financially hurt like that. What if he did it to a waitress or a shoeshine boy, or someone else? They cannot afford that sort of loss. There is just too much pain in the world."

When they returned to the *Aurora* Beatrix excused herself and went to her cabin. Even Theo realized that she was drained and hurting from the experience and didn't say anything when he collapsed into a leather chair in his brother's study. "She's right about a lot of people getting hurt."

"Well, if Haggerty did have to get himself murdered, let's hope it happened before he spread too much more of that stuff around town. I guess we'll find out soon enough. Say, you think that Miss Randall was in on this?"

Horace snorted in disgust. "Little brother, we've got more questions than answers, and none of it is making sense."

"Seems to me we kinda-sorta get more and more questions all the time," Fred added.

"You're not being helpful," Horace quietly told him. "This thing has gone from finding a body to a murder, and with Miss Randall in the midst of it, and maybe Moran's gang up here, to phoney money. Plus the street talk about a golf course."

"I think it's all related," Phoebe said, startling the three men who didn't know she was on the boat.

"Where did you come from, young lady? I thought you were going to the library. Horace asked when he looked up and saw Phoebe in the doorway. He wondered how long she had been there.

"Oh, Henry was horsing around with some other boys so I came back here to read. I borrowed one of your books while you were gone."

"What have you been reading?" her grandfather asked.

"Sherlock Holmes, what else? I've been reading the *The Adventure of the Red-Headed League,* and I just finished it."

Horace stared silently at her, and for a moment Phoebe felt she had done something wrong. Slowly, a smile began to curl up on the right side of his face. "Duplicity and subterfuge," he smiled. "Well done, Phoebs! Now, can you do something more for us? Put a book mark in the book and take it down to Doctor Howell's cabin and leave it outside the door. Don't knock. She's resting right now. But she'll see it when she gets up, and she'll read it. Thank you." Horace, Theo, and Fred watched as she hurried off on the errand.

"What's this red-headed league business? Never heard of them," Fred said.

"It's a Sherlock Holmes story about a bunch of bank robbers who wanted to hire the teller to get him out of the bank when it was closed for lunch. That way they could tunnel through the walls. To do it, they organized a club for red-headed men so they could hire just the teller without him being suspicious," Horace explained.

Fred looked perplexed and then understood. "In other words a smoke screen like we used during the war!"

"Something like that. That's what Phoebe thinks," Horace smiled thinly.

"You know, there's another little matter that hasn't been considered," Theo said, changing the subject. "Garrison hasn't released the body, but we still don't know anything about him. Haggerty, that is. We don't know who his people are, if he was married, if his parents are alive, brothers and sisters, where they live. We don't know a thing about him. Nothing, and let's face it, we don't know anything about his lady-friend, either, except what she told us, and I don't exactly trust her."

Neither Horace, nor Fred said anything.

"Phoebs, would you get that black notebook, along with my ink pen? I think we need you to start taking notes again." He got up from his desk so she could sit down to work. "Gentlemen, let's put all our questions on paper. Just the questions. When Beatrix joins us, she may have more, and by then, probably all of us.

At first their questions were random, jumping from Charlie Haggerty to Miss Randall and to others, to everything from the chain ferry and Bob Campbell to the golf bag and money. Phoebe barely managed to keep up with them as they jumped from one idea to the next, The confusion and lack of order was bewildering to her, and Fred's comments seemed to skew things up all the more. Only when she remembered to just listen and take dictation, forcing herself not to think, did she feel she was keeping up.

From the galley, Mrs. Garwood could see them working at the table, and did her part by making two pitchers of lemonade and putting thick oatmeal cookies on a platter. "I expect them to be finished," she told them when she briefly interrupted. "You need cookies to think, just like schoolboys. And, girls," she added, winking at Phoebe. Horace suggested a ten-minute break, and then they settled back to their work.

"Well, it looks like we have a long list. Let's leave it for a while. Maybe something else will come to us, and then we'll see what Beatrix says, too," Horace yawned. "I need to stretch my legs. Phoebs, you want to come along with me? I want to hear more about your thinking about the Holmes story you just read."

The two of them walked a couple of blocks down to a park bench. "You know, I think this is exactly where I was sitting when you came up to sell me some flowers," he told her.

"A dime a bunch!" she laughed.

"Best investment I ever made," he told her. "You know, we didn't realize it at the time, but you changed my life that day."

"Mine, too."

They looked at each and added, "For the better!"

"Earlier, you told me you were going to the library, but you weren't there very long. Is everything all right?" he asked.

"Wellllllllllll....I'm not sure," she said carefully.

"What happened. Didn't Henry meet you there?"

"Yes, but a few minutes later some of his friends came, and he went over to them and then they all left. I thought he liked me." Phoebe knew her grandfather had a lot on his mind and didn't want to remind him she had already told him.

"I'm sure he does, but he might be having a hard time letting you know that he likes you."

"I thought maybe he left because boys don't like smart girls," she said softly.

"Now, that is where you are very, very wrong. I'll agree, some boys and even some men don't like women they think are smarter than themselves, but they are misguided. They're not thinking straight. Maybe they're lacking in self-confidence or something. Most men like a brainy woman," Horace told her firmly.

"Is that why you like Doctor Howell, because she's smart?"

"Yes. Absolutely. In some ways she might be a lot smarter than I am, well, at least on some subjects. I'm probably better at surgery, well, at least I was. But I don't know anyone smarter in a pathology lab than Doctor Howell. And you know, you're a lot like her, so don't ever let me hear you again talk about being worried because you have a sharp brain and aren't afraid to use it," he told her firmly.

Phoebe agreed, then quickly changed the subject. "Grandfather, how come you always read the *Chicago Tribune* when you don't like Colonel McCormick? Mother won't allow the paper in the house."

"Well, that's a long story. The *Tribune* is a good paper, and you're right - I don't much care for Mr. McCormick or men like him. They think too highly of themselves and steal the credit from others."

"Is it because my father was working for him when he got killed?" she quietly asked, looking up at him.

"No," he said quickly.

Phoebe asked, "I thought you wanted to talk about the story I was reading?"

"I did. But we can always do that later. I really wanted to spend some time with you. Looks like we've gotten a bit busy with this mystery. I didn't want you feeling I was ignoring you."

She reached over to squeeze his hand. She realized he was lonely, just like he had been when they first met. "And besides, Uncle Theo and Aunt Clarice are busy with all of their Saugatuck friends. I'll bet Uncle Theo didn't tell you that he's started playing Majohng with Aunt Clarice and some other couples. Don't you want to play, too? They seem to have a lot of fun."

Horace sat on the bench, staring out across the water, for so long Phoebe began to wonder if she had been wrong to mention having fun. Her grandfather had forgotten how to play. She sat, trying to remember to sit up straight and not fidget, obeying her mother's instructions on having "Paris Manners." Horace pulled out his pipe, slowly filled it, and then struck a match before he answered, "You might be onto something. I'll have to read that story again. It was never one of my favourites, but like I said, you might be on to something. When Doctor Howell reads it, I want to read it again."

His comment confused her. They had been talking about being lonely and having fun, but he had forced the thoughts from his mind and returned to the mystery. "You just might have pointed us in the right direction, Watson."

She smiled when he called her by the name of Sherlock Holmes' friend and assistant. Maybe, just maybe, she thought, he was right about brainy girls.

CHAPTER FIFTEEN

"Fred informed me that you and Phoebe had gone for a walk. Did you put the book outside my door?" Beatrix asked. "I read the story."

"No, that was our little Miss Watson's idea. She read it and thought it might be helpful. I'm not certain, but maybe she is onto something we didn't catch," Horace said, offering her his pipe as they sat on the forward deck, looking towards the Chain Ferry as Bob Campbell cranked it to the far side.

"There are no obvious similarities, Horace," she said. "No false fraternal organizations of men with red hair, and no one is tunnelling into the Fruitgrowers Bank. I believe you are going down the proverbial blind alley. I am going to the newsstand or drug store to buy some cigars. Please come along."

"All right," he said. He was not surprised when she handed him a two dollar bill to make the purchase. Independent woman or not, she still believed there was something socially unacceptable about a woman buying cigars, and she wasn't the type to fib by saying that she was buying them for a man.

"Why do you believe that Phoebe might see something that we have missed?" she asked.

"It isn't the tale of adventure itself, so much as the idea of subterfuge and deception, all of it carefully calculated. Maybe that's what is happening here. We have too many different stories. Haggerty and Miss Randall, for starters. Then we get tales of Bugs Moran and maybe even Capone trying to pull a fast one up here with this golf club business. Oh, and let's not forget Hammer Morgan who may or may not work for Moran and may or may not even be in town. Fred has been looking for him, but he hasn't found him yet. On top of that we mix in the counterfeit money," Horace said.

"Are you saying they are or are not all related?" Beatrix asked, confused.

"Now, that's the question - are they or aren't they? And, why is Chief Garrison dragging his feet on finding Haggerty's next of kin? So, that leaves us wondering if he can be trusted or if he's up to something."

"I believe the Chief is very busy with the counterfeit money right now," Beatrix said gently.

"True. Good point, but even so, there is too much here, too many loose ends, and none of it seems to add up. When we get back, I'd like you to take a look at a list we made of all the questions we came up with. Theo and Fred agreed maybe you would find the question that is the right one. Or, maybe you'll add more to the list."

"You mean, the right answer that will solve everything like a nice neat chemical formula?" she asked.

Horace snorted. "That, too."

"I am only stating the obvious, but people do not convert into nice neat formulas. That is why I prefer chemical equations and formulas."

'Well, we'd still be grateful, I'd be grateful, if you would take a look at the list and think it over."

With a thin smile she answered, "I will."

Chief Garrison was in the drug store when Horace and Beatrix arrived, talking with an increasingly agitated pharmacist. "Look, all

I'm telling you is that it is against the law, the federal law of these here United States of America, for you to have any of that counterfeit money. You can end up in the big house if you hold on to it, and worse if you try passing it off to someone else. You understand that? So, go through your till and let's see the twenties. Now."

He had just four twenty dollar bills in his tray, and the chief inspected them carefully. "You're clean." In a little notebook he wrote that he had been to the drugstore. "Now, you might want to go through your deposit bag to make sure the money is all legit. Otherwise, if I get a report from the bank that you tried passing off some bad bills I'll run you in sure as anything! And I mean every word of it, too! And just so you don't try pulling a fast one, the tellers over to the bank will be checking, too."

The Chief wheeled around and crashed into Doctor Horace. "Well, this sure is a lot of extra work for me and my boys. I hope you're happy about it. I got more stores to check. And I've had the editor of the Commercial Record hot on my trail wanting a story. He'll probably print it on the front page under Second Coming type just to scare the bejesus out of everyone in the county. Now, unless you are going to tell me who killed Haggerty, get out of my way!"

"Nice to see you again, too, Chief," Horace snapped at him as the Chief pushed him out of his way.

"He seems very upset," Beatrix said with a half smile.

"Yes, I wonder what could have caused that?" he teased back.

Beatrix was working on the list at Horace's desk in his study, a thin whiff of smoke from her cigar trailing up from the ashtray, her untouched drink in front of her. She had asked Horace for time to work in solitude, but Phoebe was not aware of it. The girl knocked at the door and stepped into the room. At first Beatrix ignored her and then looked up.

"Just the right person at the right time. I cannot help but wonder if you are planning on becoming a physician. You have already mastered the ability to write like a doctor. Please do not take that as a compliment. I need you to explain a couple of words for me, please."

When they finished the short task, Phoebe said, "I know you are busy, but this is important. Grandfather and I were talking today about boys. Well, Henry, really. You see, I was to meet Henry at the library but when some other boys came, he went off with them. I thought it was because I'm the smartest student in our class and that it was my fault. But Grandfather said that boys like smart girls, and I, well, I think that's why he likes you so much, because you're smart, and well, that makes me happy. She quickly turned and left the room, completely interrupting Beatrix' train of thought. She stared at the door, trying to make sense of it. It didn't upset her, but neither did she quite understand what the girl meant.

Beatrix took a long puff on her cigar and barely wetted her tongue with her drink, smiled, and then went back to her work. On a separate piece of paper she rearranged some of the questions, adding a few of her own, deleting some of the repetitive ones. When she finished, she set down her pen, reread her paper, and then closed her eyes to concentrate.

It was just before dinner that she finally left the study.

CHAPTER SIXTEEN

Beatrix remained silent throughout dinner, and it was only when everyone was pushing back from the table that she asked Fred and the Balfour brothers to join her in Horace's office. "I have been thinking about the list of questions you created, and I think it is time we go to Ox-Bow and have a little talk with Miss Randall," she said firmly, "although this time I am not certain I approve of my methods."

"Want to explain that?" Horace asked.

"Very simply, after looking at the list of names that are associated with this mystery, Miss Randall is the weakest link in the chain. We will get nothing out of Chief Garrison, I prefer to avoid Hammer Norton at all costs, assuming he even exists, and that leaves Miss Randall," she explained.

"What methods are you talking about?" Theo asked.

"I believe the mob slang is, 'lean hard on her' or something like that. I do not mean in a physical sense, of course, but perhaps reasonably frighten her into talking."

"Hey, that's swell. I like that idea!" Fred said brightly.

"Very well. Gentlemen, I suggest you arm yourselves. I do not believe there will be any violence, but, perhaps a slight hint and display might convince her that we mean business. I also believe that after a day of holding a pose as a figure model, she might be quite weary."

They pulled into the parking lot just in time to see Miss Randall step out of the Old Inn. "We'd like to talk with you, Miss Randall," Horace said in the tone of voice he had used giving orders in the army or the operating room. It didn't leave room for objection. "Back inside," Horace growled at her as they led the woman to a quiet corner of the front porch. "Sit down!" he told her, then nodded at Beatrix.

"We will come straight to the point, Miss Randal. I am not certain if you are aware that Charlie Haggerty was carrying a large amount of counterfeit bills. You pointed out that he always used a new twenty dollar bill, even for a small purchase. He was passing off those bills to unsuspecting people. We also found his stash.

"Whether you knew or not is immaterial to us," Beatrix told her. "However, Chief Garrison is now aware of it, and I, that is we, believe that one of Mr. Moran's underlings is in town for that reason. That makes you an accessory after the fact, and you could get ten years for that. So far, the Chief has not set his sights on you because he is preoccupied with more urgent matters, but that is only a matter of time. And if Mr. Moran's men know that you are in the area, they will come looking for you."

"Which means if the Chief finds you first you will be arrested for counterfeiting, or at least as an accessory. You will be in jail, and if you are found guilty, sent to prison for a very long time. Counterfeiting is a federal crime," Horace added.

"And if Moran's boys get ahold of you, you're going to end up just like Charlie Haggerty - dead as a doornail," Fred snarled at her.

"So, I believe you have a choice to make, and you need to decide your future. You can come clean with us and talk, or your future is bleak," Theo said softly. "Life, prison, or dead. Which do you want?"

Miss Randall glared at them. "I don't know nothin' about any phoney money! I didn't have nothin' to do with anything like that. I just wanted a good time. Leave me out of it."

Horace stared at her, pulling out his pipe and filling it, never taking his eyes off of her. His long silence and ceaseless stare made her shiver. After he lit it and took a couple of puffs, he said quietly, "Perhaps you would like to see if there is something that you can remember that will save your life."

"I don't know nothin' I tell you! You gotta believe me!" she wailed. "You got no proof!"

"The problem, Miss Randall, is that we do not believe you," Beatrix said.

"You assume we have told you everything we know," Theo said in a quiet voice. "Are you still sure you want to take that risk?"

Miss Randall said nothing.

"We have given her an opportunity," Beatrix said to the three men. "Fred, back the car up over here, please. We're going to go for a ride."

"You thinking down along the lake where there are some ravines?" Horace asked.

Miss Randall's face drained of color. Beatrix and Horace realized she knew she had heard that phrase about taking a ride and knew what it meant. She was shaking in fear, when she realized they meant business.

"You work for Capone, don't you? Yeah, that's it! You work for Scarface!" she hissed angrily at them.

"Truth of the matter is, my brother and I have never met the man. Our dealings are with Frank Nitti. And we all know that it's Nitti who does Mr. Capone's dirty work, don't we? As my brother said, maybe we haven't told you everything we know. Now you know a little more, but not quite everything." Horace turned to Fred. "Don't forget to take Doctor Howell's medical bag out of the trunk."

"Got it boss," Fred smiled.

"You killed Charlie!" she hissed at Beatrix. "You did it! And I thought me and you were pals!"

Beatrix looked at her and said in a low serious voice, "That was your mistake. We were never pals." She nodded to Fred to get the car. "You have less than half a minute to start singing, and it had better be a good song." Beatrix posed, then said quietly, "It had better be the right song this time."

"All right, all right! I'll talk," said Miss Randall in desperation.

"Fred, sit!" Beatrix commanded. "Don't waste our time, Miss Randall."

"Lay off me, will you? I'll tell you everything I know. Look, Charlie would come into the club and I stepped out with him a couple of times. You know, just for a good time. And then one afternoon when I got there, the manager and his boss, Hammer Norton, told me they liked it I was Charlie's girl. I told them I wasn't his girl, and Hammer said that I was, and patted me on the cheek, gentle-like and gave me a big smile."

"You got in over your head," Horace told her. "I know what that cheek tapping business means, don't I?

"Yeah, no kidding I knew I was in the hot seat. And when Charlie said he was coming up here for the weekend Hammer said I was going along and that Charlie would show me a good time."

"Which is it? You came to help Charlie hang paper or set him up for a hit?" Beatrix asked. "Keep talking or Fred gets the car."

"Neither. You gotta believe me. I did what the boss told me. That's when I knew Charlie was no good, but I didn't know about the money, and I didn't set him up."

"You told me that he always pulled out a brand new twenty dollar bill when he bought something, and you told me you thought it was odd. So don't give me this malarkey about not knowing what he was doing," Beatrix snapped at her. "Try again. You're wasting my time."

"I'm telling you, I knew he was no good, but I was scared to say anything to anybody. Anyways, you're the ones who did Charlie in, not me."

All of them were silent until Beatrix stood up. "You carrying, Fred?" she asked.

"I sure am, Doc," he smiled. He pulled out his revolver and smiled.

"Keep an eye on her while I talk to my boys. Horace, Theo, let's get some fresh air," Beatrix told them.

They walked over to the car. "I'm giving her a little time to think," Beatrix whispered. "Meanwhile, what do you think?"

"I'm beginning to believe her," Horace said.

"Yeah. A young woman in the big city and with big dreams. She got in way too deep," Theo agreed. "The question is what to do with her."

"I say we take her into town and hand her over to the police. We can't leave her out here because it isn't safe, and she's likely to bolt," Horace said.

"Do you think she'll be safe in jail?" Beatrix said.

"To be honest, I'm not certain. A small town jail like that won't be much of a challenge to Moran's men. Even if they don't break in, they could poison her food. But even if Garrison's crooked, he won't want someone killed in his own jail," Horace said. "He'll do what it takes to keep her safe."

"Especially if she is in his jail," Theo added. "So what do we tell Garrison?"

"Just that we brought in Haggerty's co-conspirator in passing the counterfeit twenties. That's probably the only thing he has on his one-track mind right now. He'll arrest her and then question her later. Meanwhile, she's safe," Horace said.

"Safe, and if she is indeed involved with Haggerty's death, she won't be running off," Beatrix said. "What a sad state of affairs. I hate to say it, but I agree with you; she is better off in jail."

When they returned to the front porch, Beatrix told Fred, "Go ahead and bring the car up. Back it up to the door facing out." She looked at Miss Randall who was shaking in fear.

"Where are you taking me?" she asked.

"We're taking you for a ride," Beatrix answered flatly.

Tears came to Miss Randall's eyes and she was whimpering. "Look, I've told you everything. I didn't even want to come up here but Hammer made me do it."

"Maybe, maybe not," Theo said quietly. He nodded toward the waiting car and added, "Let's go."

Chief Garrison was just returning to the police station when Fred pulled the car up to the front. "Evening, Chief," Horace said as he stepped onto the sidewalk. "We've got a guest to stay at your luxury hotel."

"I could pack the place with three or four more others. All of them had counterfeit bills. What do you got?" the Chief asked.

"Miss Randall. I don't think she had anything to do with Haggerty's death, but she's probably an accomplice with the counterfeit notes. More than likely, an accomplice after the fact."

"Yeah? Well, that's pretty thin, if you ask me," the Chief said.

"I agree. But here's our line of thinking. The town is in an uproar by now over this. No telling what will happen tomorrow when the bank opens. You and I have seen runs on a bank that busted them over things like this. Now, if you arrest her and lock her up, and get the word out that you've made an arrest but can't talk about it, you'll be doing a lot of good," Horace explained.

Garrison thought about it, then smiled. "I can see your line of thinking, and it makes a lot of sense. I lock her up and it takes some of the pressure off everyone."

"And a lot better than locking up someone from town, if you ask me," Theo added.

"Just let her stew for a couple of days and maybe she'll have a lot more to stay. Let's face it, counterfeiting is a federal charge and she could get sent up the river for a long time. Tell her that and let her think about it for a day or two."

The Chief nodded in agreement and ordered Miss Randall into the building. "I'm holding you on suspicion of suspicious behavior and passing bad money."

When they got back in the car, Horace chuckled, "Suspicion of suspicious behavior? I've never heard that one before."

"Horace, I do not believe that is a legitimate charge," Beatrix said.

"I doubt anyone else has ever heard of it before," he chuckled again. "At least it puts Miss Randal out of harm's way for a while. And we can enjoy a peaceful night."

Clarice was waiting for them to return, a yellow envelope in her hand. "The Western Union boy just brought this for you, and you just missed the bank president," she told them.

Beatrix shuddered. "Telegrams are never good news. What is it?"

"Arriving tomorrow. Stop. Hagen and Sarazen in tow. Stop. It's from the bank cashier," Horace read the message out loud for them, then looked up. "The timing isn't the best. Now, what did the banker have to say?"

Clarice explained, "Apparently the president got the same message, and said he was likely to be very busy tomorrow. He also wants his cashier at the bank right away. It's up to us to show the two men around the area so they can see what the area has to offer."

"Thunderation!" Horace thundered.

"Grandfather, can I help?" Phoebe asked.

Horace was about to snap at her not to interfere, but instantly backed down. "Yes, yes you can! If they want to take a ride on the chain ferry or have ice cream, you're in charge." He pulled out a trio of two dollar bills. "That should about cover your expenses. Thank you for offering."

"Grandfather, is this real money?" she asked. He assured her it was.

"And Phoebe, because it is important to make a very good impression, please do not encourage them to drink a Green River phosphate if you go to the drug store. I think they are very foul," Beatrix said.

"And how!" Phoebe answered.

"Well, I like them!" Horace retorted.

"Yes, I know. By the way, Phoebe tells me you also like brainy women. It is a good thing you have at least one redeeming feature," she teased.

Beatrix smiled at Phoebe and gave her a wink. The moment of pleasure was over and the life seemed to drain out of her face. Beatrix left the others, went into Horace's study to retrieve the remains of her cigar, and walked to the bow and leaned against the rail looking at the water. Horace gave her a few minutes and then joined her.

"Have we done the right thing, Horace? Have we?" she asked quietly.

"I think so. At the very least, we did what we truly believed best."

"Horace, I terrified Miss Randall. That troubles me greatly. There is so much pain and I have added to hers....." her voice trailed away.

"I think it had to be done. We needed her to talk, and we needed her moved somewhere safe. Maybe it scared her, but she's safe for the time being. And, if she did have a hand in Haggerty's murder, then she needs to be in the lock-up."

"I know, but I was brutal to her," Beatrix said after slowly blowing a stream of smoke.

"I thought it was sheer brilliance letting her think you were part of the Chicago mob. It worked, and that's what's important. You almost had me convinced."

She suddenly turned to him. "Horace, I promise, I will never do anything like that to you. I promise!"

Horace smiled, "That's old news. I know you wouldn't. Nor I to you."

To his surprise, she moved slightly closer to him, their shoulders touching as they looked at the water. "I understand why you like to be on the water." She became silent again, and when she finished her cigar, flicked it into the river and told him she was retiring for the night.

CHAPTER SEVENTEEN

"Time to go, Phoebs. You and Fred should get on the road if you're going to be at the station ahead of the train," Horace told her early the next morning after they had finished breakfast.

"I know, the only way to be sure you are on time is to be there ten minutes early," she said, and rolled her eyes in mock boredom, repeating one of his favorite sayings whenever they were going anywhere and he was impatient.

"Just relax, remember your "Paris Manners" and be yourself. And Phoebs, you look very nice in that dress. You'll do just fine, so be confident. We're all confident you can do this job."

"Thank you," she said, blushing slightly at the compliment. She was very surprised when her grandfather had asked her to greet the visiting golfers. That was something grown-ups ordinarily did, and usually children were not included. She was being treated as an adult, a grown-up, and part of their world. When she had asked for an explanation, he simply said that the car would be too crowded if he went along, reminding her that there would be three passengers plus Fred.

Horace watched as his granddaughter and Fred got in the car. He laughed when he saw Fred grandly open up the rear passenger door for her, bowing slightly as she stepped inside. "You can sit in front on the way back, but not now. You're the lady of the morning," he told her.

To her relief and joy, they arrived in plenty of time, and she was certain that the introductions and welcome had gone smoothly. Even the anxious bank cashier was put at ease, and gladly let her do some of the talking. Phoebe had pointed out some of the important things to see, and asked Fred to drive slowly into town so they could see everything. "And over there is the Big Pavilion which is always crowded when there is a good band," she had said. The two men seemed impressed. They dropped the cashier off in front of the bank and then went on to the *Aurora* where Doctor Theo and Clarice were standing next to her grandfather and Beatrix to welcome them aboard.

"Permission to come aboard, sir?" Mr. Hagen had asked.

"Absolutely, permission granted, and welcome," Horace answered with a smile and a firm handshake to both men. When Beatrix, Theo and Clarice led their guests into the lounge, Horace turned to Phoebe and whispered, "How did it go?"

"Aces," she whispered back. "Swell. They are very nice men."

"I knew it would. I have absolute confidence in you!"

Phoebe couldn't wait for the next opportunity to help her grandfather.

"I am sure that my granddaughter gave you the cook's tour of town," Horace said as he sat down to join them.

"She did. You're a fortunate man, Doctor Balfour. She's quite the charmer," Mr. Sarazen told the group, making Phoebe blush just a little. Noticing her discomfort, Beatrix asked if she would tell Mrs. Garwood that coffee and donuts would be welcome.

"I don't know if the fellow from the bank explained that we're not really part of the investment group," Horace said. "In fact, none of us are even golfers. But, we do like Saugatuck, and we want to see it thrive. If the backers of the plan believe that it is a good thing for the village to have a golf club, then we want to do our part to support it.

"And, just so you don't get your hopes up too high, neither of us is in a position to do much more than look the place over. Golf is increasingly popular, and maybe a course is a good match for the area, or maybe not," Sarazen said.

"Or, maybe not right now," Hagen added. "There are a lot of things to be considered. Do you know what the investors have in mind?"

"Not really," Theo said. "I assume it would be a golf course and a clubhouse."

Both men were quiet. "Well, if what they want to do is have a course, and don't have unrealistic ambitions, then if they can get the land and build it, it's a lot of work. And if they have aspirations of having tournaments here, then it is a lot of work and a lot of money just to get started. I doubt there would be a quick return on their investment. It might take years, and there's the challenge the way Wall Street is climbing. If I had that sort of money, I'd want to put it there," Hagen said.

"I can see that," Horace said.

"There's something else I'll tell you and anyone else. Golf is a special game. It's not just hitting a ball and getting it into the cup. It's scrupulously clean," Hagen added.

"Clean? In what way?"

"Look, it's the only game where the players police themselves. No umpires, no referees, no one but the golfer polices himself. It's a clean, honest game played by clean honest men and women," Sarazen added.

"Clean in what way?" Beatrix asked.

"Honesty and high standards. Look, let's say you knock your ball into the rough. There's no one watching if you move your ball a little to get a better shot. Touch the ball with your club and an honest man will declare it a stroke. A crook will not.

"I'm sure you heard of Bobby Jones. He was playing in a tournament and no one but Jones knew that he had accidently touched the ball with his club. He called it, and it cost him winning the game, the trophy, and the prize money. That's the standard by which we live. We don't want cheaters around. We won't tolerate them. A cheater is black-balled from playing. Simple as that," Hagen said firmly. "No cutting corners or jay-walking through a game."

"There's something else," Sarazen added. "We don't stand for wagering. No reputable club allows it among the players or the caddies. Period. And no wagering on tournaments, either. Someone gets found out for placing a bet, and they're through. Like Walt said, Bobby Jones set the standard, and we're going to keep it that way. Boxing is crooked, the tracks are notorious for fixed races. There's betting on football and lacrosse and everything else. You remember the White Sox of 1919? One man, a fellow named Myron Wolfsheim out of New York City fixed the World Series. One man corrupted the whole of baseball. They might call him 'The Brain' and maybe he is, but golf is clean. End of story."

"I heard Grantland Rice say that if it hadn't been for Babe Ruth baseball would be dead by now. So, I take it that includes the backers of a course?" Horace asked.

"There's no secret about that. We have our own private eye to investigate anyone fronting the money. If there is someone crooked in the combine, then that's it. There won't be a tournament held there, and that's a death knell for a big club. There was a place over in Illinois where one of the Chicago gangsters got involved and put a speakeasy and casino in the basement of the clubhouse. No professional golfer is ever going there. They wouldn't dare even drive in the front gate. You get our drift?"

"We certainly do," Beatrix said. "I trust you will make that equally clear when you meet with the bank president."

Both Hagen and Sarazen chuckled. "You can count on it. We'll tell him, same as we told the cashier and we told you. You can't bet on it, but trust me; you can count on it," Hagen said.

"You folks have any idea where they are thinking of building the course?" Sarazen asked.

"None," Theo said. "Like my brother said, we don't even play the game."

"It might be helpful if we got the lay of the land, even if you don't know where they want to build," Sarazen said.

Beatrix brightened and suddenly spoke up. "Perhaps you would like a bird's eye view?"

Sarazen beamed. "You mean from the air?"

"That would be the preferred method. Yes," she replied.

"Doctor Howell has her own plane," Horace explained.

"You know, sister, I've done a lot of things in my life, but I've never gone up in an airplane. If you're offering, I'm accepting," Sarazen said.

Beatrix's eyes lit up. "In that case, to use the modern phrase, let's 'Twenty-three ski-doo.'" She stood up, ready to leave.

"Now?" Sarazen asked.

"Yes. Why not? I suggest you do it before you change your mind. Even Horace has been up with me."

"She does know how to fly, doesn't she?" Sarazen asked Horace.

"One-eyed Wiley Post gave me my first lesson, back in Minnesota," Beatrix said before Horace could answer

"I hope Gene knows what he's doing," Hagen said as they stood at the edge of the field, watching as his friend tightened his leather flying helmet and climbed into the plane.

"Probably not, but the important thing is that Doctor Howell knows what *she* is doing. He's in for an experience. Look, don't worry. She's as good as they come. Lindy can't hold a candle to her.

They watched as Beatrix taxied to the far end of the field, letting the engine warm, until she revved it up to full speed. She checked the flaps one final time. "I take it you've known each other a while," Hagen asked hopefully.

"The four of us were in school together. The three of us and Theo's wife, Clarice. She, Theo, and I became physicians. She's a pathologist, we went into surgery. Yeah, we've known her quite a while. Fred, my driver, has been with me since France in 1918.

Beatrix roared down the grass field and lifted off, buzzing over their heads, causing Hagen to drop flat on the ground. He got up and brushed himself off. "Thought she was going to hit us," he apologized.

"Ah, Doc Howell wouldn't-a done that on account of the fact that it would dent the propeller," Fred teased. "Everyone knows you can't fly with a dented propeller."

Beatrix flew over the city, banking to fly over the nearby farms while Sarazen looked at the ground below, trying to see some spots that would be possible golf courses. Just before they returned, she started to climb higher and made several wide circles, then descended. Suddenly she climbed up again for a final circle to the mouth of the Kalamazoo River. Somewhere over the lake she turned again to come low over the river and Saugatuck before landing.

"You find anywhere good?" Hagen asked after his friend and pulled off his helmet and handed it to Fred.

"Yeah, yeah, but there's something else even better. It's like this, every time she went up hard and fast, the back of the plane felt like it was falling lower. Ah, I'm not explaining it right, but the front went up and the back end dipped, if you get my meaning. It gives me an idea that if you put a little extra weight on the back end of a mashie, it might give the ball more of a lift," Sarazen said excitedly.

"Yeah, well that and a nickel will get you a cup of coffee. Never mind the tinkering, what about some good sites?" Hagan asked.

"Plenty of them. Big farm fields, some nice hills. There are plenty of places. When we came up along the river there's one between the river and the lake not far from that bridge. That place would be aces for a golf club course. Nice rolling hills down to a ravine. It'd be challenging if it's designed right."

Mr. Sarazen turned to Beatrix. "That was something! I might give up golf and take up flying. Nothing like it. I don't know why I didn't do that earlier, a long time ago. You gotta tell me more about your plane and where I get one and where I find someone to teach me!"

Beatrix was almost giddy. "Perhaps we can go up tomorrow."

"Wish we could, but we're leaving tomorrow. Say, what about this afternoon?"

"Gene, that's not what we're here for. We got to meet the bankers this afternoon," Hagen told him.

"Can't you do that without me? If Doctor Howell wants to go up this afternoon, I'll go with her."

"You're keeping your feet on the ground, pal. We made a promise. Both of us. Sorry."

"Perhaps next time you come here," Beatrix said, still smiling.

Theo nudged Horace. "You better take up flying or you'll lose your girl," he teased. Horace ignored him.

"Listen, Gene, we got to get back to that ship and get cleaned up if we're talking with bankers," his friend said. "And don't get any fancy ideas about how you could make Doc Balfour's boat into one of those aircraft carriers, either. I know how you think. We gotta focus on business now."

Horace tapped his knife against his water glass to get everyone's attention before dinner. "Gentlemen, I believe you are in for a real treat. Michigan is famous for its whitefish, and I have come to realize that it makes a mighty fine meal. That is due primarily to the clear waters but above all expertise of Mrs. Garwood. Through many trials and a few errors, she has perfected our dinner, and there is none finer anywhere up and down the coast than we'll be enjoying. Ready when you are, Mrs. G."

"You're having beef tonight," she said firmly.

"Thunderation! What in the name of Lister and Pasteur happened?" he asked.

"That whitefish that my man brought home was old and didn't smell very good. Unless you want to follow the good book where it says doctors heal yourselves, I had to throw it back into the river.

You'd all get sick. You're having beef, baked potatoes, and the last of the beets," she answered back.

"Thunderation! I have been thinking about whitefish all afternoon. Why didn't you send the captain out for more?" Horace snarled.

"I did just that, and guess what? There aren't more whitefish this side of the lake, leastwise not around here. The Odd Fellows are having a big fish fry tonight. I heard it was special doings up at their lodge, and they bought it all. Just be grateful he found some good beef or you'd be having the vegetable plate tonight."

"Thunderation!"

To make matters worse, Beatrix had to hold her napkin up to her face to mask her laughter.

"Say, I just had an idea. If those Odd Fellows are having a special goings-on, and seeing how I'm a member and all, maybe I ought to scoot over there and see if I can pick up anything useful... for our project, that is." Fred said, pushing back his chair.

"Fred, if we're not having whitefish, neither are you. That was the lamest excuse I've heard of. Stay right where you are. Thunderation!"

Beatrix was joined by Clarice and Harriet, holding their napkins to hide their laughter. Only Phoebe remained stone-faced, and only because she was in sympathy with her grandfather.

"Listen Doc, that's what my ma would call a blessing in disguise," Mr. Hagen said. "See, when we were in Traverse City, they didn't feed us anything but whitefish for three days running, lunch and dinner, and cherry pie for dessert. They even had a whitefish omelette on the breakfast menu. Right now beef seems awfully good to us, don't it, Walter?"

"I'm with you on that one," Mr. Sarazen replied. "Beef seems pretty tasty to me tonight. And I'm grateful for a plate of shoe leather as long as it's home-cooked."

"You see?" asked a very miffed Mrs. Garwood. "They know how to appreciate a good meal. And it won't be shoe leather, either, that comes from my kitchen."

"Thunderation!" Horace muttered. "Three years I've been coming here, and not once has she served whitefish."

"I thought you said through trial and error?" Sarazen asked.

"Yes, and I was being optimistic. Three years I've been trying to get her to cook just one meal of whitefish, and for three years she's made an error in getting it from the kitchen to the table. She's perfected that part, all right," he growled.

Beatrix kept her napkin in front of her face, focusing on controlling her breathing so that she did not break out laughing. She watched in relief as Mrs. Garwood left the room to return to her galley, and came back with a large serving platter. Horace's eyes narrowed as he watched her set it in front of him to serve his guests.

"Mrs. G, this is not beef! It's whitefish!" he said, confused at what had just happened.

"Oh, so it is. My, miracles still happen," she laughed at the prank she had just played.

"Horace, before you say anything, I set this up. Mrs. Garwood went along with the joke," Beatrix said brightly. "It is rather amusing, is it not?"

He was dumb-founded and couldn't find the right words.

"Mrs. G, I believe I owe you this scarf that the captain said you had been eying in the store window," Beatrix said in triumph, handing her a small package. "Do enjoy wearing it, and may you think of how you succeeded in surprising Horace!"

If anything, Theo looked even more surprised than Horace. It wasn't about their dinner, but the realization that Beatrix had a sense of humour. "Well done, Beatrix!" He lifted his water glass. "You sure got the old man!"

Horace recovered quickly. "Well, the joke is on me. And you know what, after we finish this meal, so is the ice cream! And an extra scoop for you, Beatrix, and the Garwoods."

"Well, gentlemen, what do you think of Saugatuck now that you've been here?" Theo asked when he and Horace accompanied the two golfers back to the train station.

"Nice little place. Real nice. But your real question is about a golf course, and I don't know what to tell you. The bank president has some good ideas, and he said he's got some backers lined up, but he didn't want to give up the names. At some point, he'll have to come forward with that. But I'll tell you what else I think. If you folks want a golf course here, then build it for yourselves. Start small. If it's a good course and if people come, then it will grow. Have a plan that's reasonable run it like a business. An honest business, remember! There've been too many that started out big and couldn't make a go of it. And that's when it either folds or the criminal element tries to worm their way in," Sarazen said.

"Good advice," Theo said. "We'll pass it along."

CHAPTER EIGHTEEN

"Well, I'd say that eliminates both Bob Campbell and the golf course from our list of suspects," Horace said when he and Beatrix went for a walk after lunch. "Not much progress, is it?"

"Yes, I believe you are right. Golf has always been something I cannot understand. There seems to be little purpose in hitting a little white ball and then going walking after it to hit it again, just to knock it into a little cup in the ground. It seems too foolish and such a waste of time," Beatrix said.

"There was a time when I wanted to pick up the game," Horace said quietly, the memory of it coming back to him.

"Yes, and I remember exactly what your mother told you. "You want to walk on the grass behind something, push the lawn mower and get the grass cut before your father gets home.""

They both chuckled, but then Beatrix did the unexpected. She turned to Horace and asked, "Maybe you should have played golf. You never learned how to have fun."

"Now, that's where you're wrong. I do have fun. I just happen to believe that work is the best kind of fun," he told her, trying to brush off some of the pain.

"Perhaps we could try having fun together, sometime. Not today, but sometime," she suggested.

"Right now, solving this mystery is my idea of fun. We'll do that first, and then think of something." He looked over at two young girls playing hopscotch on the sidewalk. For a moment he considered telling Beatrix that being with her was what he really enjoyed, but he hesitated, uncertain how she might respond. "We could try that sometime," he suggested once the girls had finished playing and moved on.

"Why?" she asked. "It appears to be a highly over-rated experience."

Horace surprised himself and led her over to the chalk boxes drawn on the sidewalk. He picked up the pebble and rolled it, then hopped from one square to the next. In triumph he turned, picked up the stone and handed it to her, and she made her way down the frame.

"You're right. It is a highly over-rated experience," Horace teased. "If we find an old can, perhaps we can see if kicking it down the street is better." His comment was rewarded with her look of disdain.

With the idea of finding something fun to do forgotten by mutual consent, they continued walking down to the north end of Water Street, then they turned, and walked back down Butler, eventually stopping at the bank.

"So far, we've found twenty-seven of those counterfeit twenties," the president told Horace and Beatrix. "We didn't have to do it, not by law, anyway, but we've made restitution for all of them."

"Five hundred forty dollars is a lot of money," Horace said.

"It is, but the bank can afford it. Some of our clients can't. That's probably more than the shoeshine boy down to Dominck's makes in a week or two. Or the carry out-boy over at the store, and a lot of others. That just wouldn't have been fair for them to suffer."

"That is very generous of you," Beatrix said quietly. "Do you see any pattern to it - to the people who received the bogus money?"

The banker laughed. "Chief Garrison was here not half an hour ago asking the same question. Neither of us saw any sort of a pattern. It looks like it was random. The rough part is, we don't know when it started, other than sometime over the weekend. And if there is a bright spot, it doesn't look like it's still going on. Seems to have come to a stop."

"Well, that's something, at least," Horace said. "Well, let us know if you uncover anything, would you? Did anyone happen to remember where they got the bad bills, who gave it to them?

The banker snorted. "Nope. Complete blank."

"That's about what I would have expected," Horace said. "Well, see you in the funny papers."

As soon as they were out of the bank Beatrix asked, "You expected everyone to forget. That seems odd."

"Not at all. Anyone who turned in a counterfeit bill had probably been warned by the Chief that they could be arrested. That's for starters. And second, it all happened over a busy weekend. Money coming into town, changing hands. This is their busy season, so the merchants and others were eager to get the money, and didn't check it over. That, and they were busy keeping an eye on the till to make sure their employees weren't dipping in and helping themselves. To top it off, I'll bet some of them felt pretty embarrassed that they got taken. So, there you have it - a case of mass amnesia."

"I see," she said quietly. "It is not very logical. If they would be more forthcoming the police could find the, I believe the term you used was 'paper-hanger.'"

"People are rarely logical. Sometimes, Beatrix, I really do envy you working in a lab and not having to deal with patients and their

don't mean to lie, but they don't like to open up too ... re scared. Same thing. A lot of scared people."

"...., . where Phoebs is, Mrs. G?" Horace asked when they returned to the boat.

"She sweet-talked Fred into going out and driving around to look for a brown car. That girl doesn't fall far from the tree, does she? One year it was learning how to be a radio operator, the next it's the piano, and this year, it's brown cars," Mrs. Garwood said.

"That's my granddaughter," he told her, with a smile. He walked back to where Beatrix was leaning against the rail to look at the river. "She and Fred are out. The official story is that they are looking for the mysterious brown car. My guess is that she talked him into giving her a driving lesson."

"Do you think she would like me to teach her?" she asked.

"She probably would prefer it was teaching her how to fly." Horace shook his head and rolled his eyes.

"Perhaps she would go up with me and look for the brown car from the air. She could be a spotter," Beatrix offered.

"We'll keep that in mind for the future. I'm going to be in enough hot water when her mother finds out we've been teaching her to drive."

"Yes. Yes, I can see that potentially being the result."

They leaned on the rail, idly looking at the river and a couple of small sailboats that went past them. Horace pulled out his pipe and lit it. "There is nothing as peaceful as watching a river," he said quietly.

Minutes passed before she responded.

"Horace, it just occurred to me that there is something unusual at the Butler Hotel," she said quietly, carefully thinking through her words.

"Such as?"

"The bellboy. For the past few days there is a new one. Do you not find that unusual?" she asked.

"Not really. Bellboys come and go. They quit, they get fired, they get a better paying job at a big hotel. Or maybe Cal had a day or so of vacation."

"Not always. The desk clerk at the Palmer House called one for Clarice and me, and he said he had been there since the place was built," Beatrix objected. "I believe that might have been an exaggeration."

"That makes sense that he'd be there for the long run. A big hotel in a big city. They get decent wages and good tips. No wonder they stay. Don't get me wrong, but the Butler Hotel isn't like the Palmer House."

"Perhaps you will tell me it is a wild goose chase, but it may be important." She turned and started to walk across the deck before turning again. "Horace, are you coming?"

"The manager just stepped out," the clerk explained. "You can wait in the lobby if you like. It shouldn't be more than a few minutes." Horace and Beatrix found a small table and chairs at the far end of the room.

"Yeah, that's right. Cal's been with us for about five years. I gotta tell you, he isn't any too bright, but he's polite and a steady worker," the manager said when he sat to join them. "Leastwise, he was."

"Where is he now?" Horace asked.

"You tell me and then we'll all know. The other morning he didn't turn up. I drove over to Douglas to a place he rents, a rooming house, but there wasn't hide nor hair of him. Nothing. Like I said, he isn't too bright, so I figured maybe someone had said something to him, or I don't know. Anyway, I'm beginning to think he left us."

"By any chance, do you still owe him any of his wages?"

The manager snorted. "That's the rum thing. He took off and I owe him for three days work. It's odd that he'd leave, and odder that he'd walk out on some of his money."

"When was that?" Beatrix asked.

"Oh, that's an easy one. Same day that this Charlie Haggerty got himself killed. A fellow isn't likely to forget that day, especially seeing how he was a guest here."

"One more question, if you don't mind," Horace asked. "After Cal quit and disappeared, what did you do? Did you inform Chief Garrison."

"Well, I tried to, but he was busy with the murder. And he said that Cal was of age and if he wanted to quit there wasn't anything he could do to make him come back to work. You know what the Chief is like."

"So, that leaves you short-handed," Horace said.

"Say, I got lucky on that one. A couple of hours after Cal didn't show up for work a fellow walks in here, says he's from Detroit and used to work at a hotel, and wants to know if I had anything for him. Well, he was about the same size as Cal so he'd fit the uniform, so I hired him. He does okay. Sort of quiet and keeps to himself, but he knows how to carry a bag and he's polite. Say, I'd like to sit here a while longer, but now's the time we get ready for the evening rush."

On their walk back Beatrix asked, "Your thoughts?"

"It could be a coincidence. A low paid employee walks out, a fellow comes in a couple of hours later looking for work and gets hired. I don't see what this has to do with the murder," Horace said flatly.

"I do not believe in coincidences. Have you ever read Einstein's theory of general relativity?" she asked.

"No. Physics doesn't make a good match with surgery."

"If everything is related, then there are not coincidences in the universe. Now, I will not go so far as to say I believe what the university chaplain taught, that there are no coincidences but only God moments. But I believe its consideration is warranted in this situation."

"Fill your boots, Beatrix, but when we get back to the boat I'm going to do some flat work," Horace told her.

"Flat work? What is that?" she asked.

"I'm going to stretch out flat on my back on my bunk and examine the inside of my eyelids," he told her.

"I believe that is a wise decision. You need a nap. We need to stop at the drugstore," she said, reaching into her handbag for a dollar bill."

"Cigars?" he asked.

"Cigars. And then I will be in your study. When you awaken come and join me. By then I may have some theories."

"And feel free to help yourself...."

"Thank you," she said. "If you do not object, should Fred return before you awaken, I would like to ask him to go to his usual haunts and find out anything about Cal the bellboy."

"Sure. Just don't take Phoebe up in your plane. Promise?" he yawned.

"Promise."

Horace yawned again. "There's something I can't figure out. A counterfeiting job takes a lot of expertise and time to do, and that means a lot of money. Whoever passed those bills must have been a rank amateur, and they took a lot of risks of getting caught for next to nothing. It doesn't add up. I'm not certain we're on the right track trying to tie all of it up into one nice neat bundle, despite Einstein's theory."

CHAPTER NINETEEN

Horace awoke with a start, and for a few moments was a bit disoriented and confused. Fred was urgently tapping at his cabin door. "Wakey-wakey, General! Gown and mask time! Duty calls!" The words left him thinking he was back in France at an army hospital.

"What?" he demanded when he pulled open the door.

"They just brought in a fellow in rough shape. Doctor Landis sent for you two and Doctor Howell. He needs you in a hurry. Doc Howell has your bag, and your brother is already on deck. Begging your pardon, General, but shake a leg."

Horace quickly pulled on his shoes and followed behind Fred out to the car. "What do we know?" Theo asked.

"Not much," Fred told him. "Some people found this fellow halfway out the crawl space under that red chapel over on the other side of the river, right near the lake. They thought he was a goner, but then they found a pulse and hauled him to the hospital."

"Very brave of them," Horace said.

"I understand it was a man and wife out of St. Louis, and he'd been in the war, so there you have it," Fred answered. "And before you ask, I don't know much more on account of the fact that he's unconscious and in bad shape."

Horace whispered, "Thunderation," when he saw the patient. "Looks rough. I'm surprised he's lasted this long."

"No kidding," Doctor Landis said. "Broken bones from the jaw all the way down, and no telling what else. He looks like he's going into shock. I haven't had time to examine much more. Probably internal bleeding. You two had better take the lead on this."

Horace nodded silently in agreement

Beatrix had immediately gone to the top of the examination table. "I think his neck has been damaged. We've got to stabilize that before he moves around or we move him." She carefully ran her hands over the sides of his neck and up the back, then let out an audible gasp.

"What?" Theo asked.

"Same puncture wound that we found on Charlie Haggerty, only this time whoever did it missed the carotid. I'll start stabilizing his neck," she said firmly.

"Block and tackle are in the back room," Doctor Landis told her.

"Block and tackle? I am not familiar with the term," she answered.

"Everything you need to stabilize him, and the straps and bandages to tackle it into place. You need a hand, sing out," Landis told her. He nodded toward a closet door.

"Landis, see if you can stabilize him. I'd start by preparing a morphine drip, and a syringe with adrenalin in case he starts going west on us. He'll need morphine later if he pulls through. And that's a big maybe." Horace shook his head. "Theo and I'll work on his belly because there's got to be some internal bleeding. Fred, you remember how to pass gas?"

'Yes, Sir, General. Like riding a bike - you never forget."

"Good man. Now, just a light slow drip. He's fragile enough as it is. Just keep him under. No more, or we'll lose him. Get a stethoscope and keep checking his heart. When Beatrix is done with the neck, turn that over to her and help us. And go gently on his face. It looks like his left jaw is shattered."

"Yes, sir," Fred said."

As soon as the patient was anesthetized, Theo took a large gauge needle and syringe. "Let's see what his spleen has to tell us." He grunted as he pushed hard to drive the needle into the organ, paused, and began to draw out fluid. "That's our bleeder. I'll assist," he told Horace and the others. Doctor Landis brought out a surgical cart, and chuckled slightly when he said he'd "play nurse."

"No hard feelings, but my Mrs. Balfour was the best.

"None taken," Landis said good naturedly.

"You ever done that before, Doc?" Fred asked Beatrix when she returned with the equipment.

"Yes. The last time was August 17 in '94. It was, however, in the morgue," she replied flatly.

"That there being the case, and seeing as how I done did it over there in France, maybe you and I ought to switch places. I'll do the neck if you'll pass gas," Fred suggested. To his amusement, Beatrix gasped in horror at his words, then realized what he meant. She blushed furiously.

They settled into a routine and worked in near silence. Beatrix kept close watch over their patient, waiting to see if he made any movement. Each time he did, she let a couple more drops of ether fall on to the cotton mask over his face. Doctor Landis stood next to

Horace and opposite Theo as he handed them an array of medical instruments.

A hospital orderly, his hand holding a mask over his face, stuck his head in the door. "The police chief is here to talk to you. He says its important."

"Good for him. Tell him to wait until we're done here. And if he gives you any grief, tell him a man's life is at stake," Landis snapped.

"Doctors, please hurry. A sprint not a marathon. He's been under for twenty five minutes and counting. Time is of the essence," Beatrix said firmly. "His blood pressure is dangerously low."

"Got it," Horace said, not looking up. "I'm just finishing removing the spleen now." He used large forceps to lift the organ into a bowl held by Doctor Landis. "He took a real beating. I'll start suturing the bleeders. Theo, get ready to close. Landis, I need you to sponge the field to keep it dry. I don't want to miss any of the small bleeders and have to open him up again."

Horace worked quickly, with Theo removing clamps as they went along. Both men talked to themselves, raising their voices just slightly when they needed the other's attention.

"You two work like a well oiled machine," Landis said.

"Comes with a half century of practice," Horace said quietly, still focused on his work. "We've been each other's first assistants since we got out of medical school, and before that, with Father."

"I can tell."

"Count your sponges and let's close him up. How's he doing, Beatrix?"

"Steady, now that you've stopped the bleeding. Blood pressure is up, and his heart is steady. Don't slow down to do fine needlework, please, Theo."

"Sponges?" Doctor Landis gasped. "I forgot to count!"

"Fine nurse you'd make," Horace teased. "Good thing you're a doctor." He felt the abdominal cavity. "Clear. Theo, start making like a seamstress. Fred, go get four splints for his arms and legs."

"Two of each?" Fred asked.

Horace's eyes widened, "That would probably be the best idea. Yes, two of each. Thunderation! Beatrix, I think your job is done. Well done. Very well done. We'll get him splinted up, and then let's have some orderlies get him up to a room. I'd encourage you to make sure he has someone with him round-the-clock, Landis. It's your hospital, and I dislike telling you how to run it, but he'll need a good nurse."

"We'll take care of it. I've got a couple of our best in mind," Landis said. "You know, the man wouldn't be alive now if it weren't for the four of you."

"Your modesty is unbecoming. You forgot to include yourself, Landis. There were five of us, and don't forget that. Let's hope he pulls through and recovers. He's going to be your guest for a long time, I'm afraid. Listen, if it is any help, I'll see if Mrs. Balfour can spell your staff," Theo offered. "Anyone know how long we've been at this?"

"Two hours and seventeen minutes," Beatrix said wearily.

"Feels like it, too," Theo yawned. "And lucky us - we still have to see Chief Garrison." He made a face of displeasure.

"How soon can I see the fellow you just worked out?" the Chief asked.

"Good question. I wish we knew. You can see him, but he's unconscious. He was that way when he came in. He's been beaten pretty badly," Landis explained. "He's hanging on by a threat. Ruptured spleen, probably cracked ribs, and no telling what his arms and legs are like. Probably cracked neck bones, and no telling how badly his brain might be damaged. He's still out cold from the ether, and he'll be under sedation for a few days. I don't think there is any chance you'll get much out of him until then. And that's assuming he even survives."

Chief Garrison let out a low whistle. "That bad, huh? Any good news?

"Not yet, but there is more you should know. On the left side of his neck was a puncture wound that was identical to the one on Bob Haggerty. There can be little doubt that the same person or persons did it to both men," Beatrix answered

"Then how come this one is alive and Haggerty died?"

"Our patient was fortunate. The needle didn't enter the artery. In my opinion, the man was severely beaten, perhaps for information. The physical trauma is life threatening. I believe that after they were finished beating him they intended to kill him by the same means they killed Haggerty."

"I still find that hard to believe, you know?" the chief answered.

"That is understandable. However, I believe that he is in very great danger. If whoever did this finds out that he survived, they will draw a line straight to the hospital. It is my advice that you post one of your deputies outside his door for his protection, as well as for the medical staff of the hospital."

"Give him a body guard? Who is he? Someone important?" the Chief snipped. "That sort of thing costs money."

"The man's life is at stake," Horace snapped at the Chief. "And this man may be the key to solving Haggerty's murder, the counterfeit bills, and all the rest. You want to solve this, you see to it that he doesn't get killed."

"Anything else, your royal highness?" the Chief asked, looking at Beatrix

Beatrix smiled. "As a matter of fact there is. I would encourage you to go over to the Butler Hotel and arrest the bellhop."

"Calvin? What in the world for? He's all right. Why would I want to arrest Calvin?" the chief asked.

Very quietly Beatrix explained. "Calvin is the man on whom we just operated. The morning when he did not come to work, an out-of-town man turned up at the hotel looking for a job. He is the same size and approximate weight as Calvin, and the hotel hired him immediately. Perhaps it is a coincidence, but I find it highly suspicious. I am sure you will too, when you think it through."

"Calvin is in there? The operating room? Someone roughed him up?" the Chief asked.

"Roughed him up is a vast understatement," Theo said. "Nearly beat him to death."

"Calvin's never hurt anyone in his life. He's not too bright, but he's a good-natured cuss. Everyone likes him. Everyone." The Chief suddenly became silent, then asked, "You think the new bellhop has something to do with it?"

"I do," said Beatrix. "I believe the charge of suspicion of being suspicious should be adequate to arrest him."

"You bet your boots, lady, I'm going to run him in. And I'll get him to talk. I don't have to be nice about it like I am with Miss Randall. Give me five minutes alone with him and I'll get it out of him! And you'll have your bodyguard for Calvin, too. Not a person on the Village Council will raise a stink about the money it'll cost. Some of them will volunteer to keep watch, I'll betcha!"

"Listen, go easy on that bellhop would you? We've done enough surgery for one day" Landis said firmly.

"Boss, you mind much if I stick around down here until Garrison gets a deputy to take over the guard duty? Might be safer for your patient if I was to do that," Fred asked.

"That's good thinking. And kind of you," Horace said.

"You take the car, and I'll look after myself about getting back to the boat." He reached into his pocket for the key, and before anyone else could move, Beatrix had her hand out to take them. She gave the Balfours a smile and said, "I'll drive. You two are exhausted."

Theo might have been tired, but not too tired to give Horace a knowing look and a smile. Horace was tired and didn't want to admit his leg was throbbing from where he'd been wounded weeks earlier.

CHAPTER TWENTY

"That was a bit of a twist, your conversation with Chief Garrison," Horace said when they returned to the *Aurora*.

"A twist or surprise, perhaps, but a logical conclusion," Beatrix told the two brothers as they migrated to the deck chairs.

"Go on," Horace said.

"As I said earlier, I do not believe in coincidences. Charlie Haggerty and Miss Randall agree to meet in Saugatuck, and although both of them did come here, they do not meet. Charlie is killed and Miss Randall claims to know nothing about it. We find Haggerty's stash of counterfeit money and alert the bank and police. Calvin suddenly disappears, and I think we can safely say that he was kidnapped and nearly beaten to death by someone connected to this criminal enterprise. That is a logical assumption because a bellhop has ready access to all the rooms as well as the bell captain's closet. The morning that Calvin does not report for work, a complete stranger walks into the hotel asking for a job. I doubt it was any coincidence that he was the same size as Cal," Beatrix explained, ticking off each point with her fingers.

"It's still a bit of a stretch," Theo said.

Horace shook his head in disagreement. "I think you're onto something Beatrix. The man who took the bellhop job would have had the perfect opportunity to snoop around the hotel and elsewhere." He paused, his face frozen, and then he added slowly and quietly, "That could mean there was a lot more of that bogus cash than just what we found or has turned up. That would explain Calvin's troubles."

"I think so, too." She answered. "As you pointed out, it is an expensive and time-consuming task to print counterfeit money. I think either Haggerty was here or to see if he could pass it without anyone catching on, or else there is a big stash of it we have not yet found."

"You're forgetting another possibility," Theo added. "What if Haggerty stole the counterfeit money, and whoever bumped him off came looking for it?"

"That is certainly worthy of serious consideration," she answered.

"Fine, but then what about Bob Campbell, the brown Buick, and going off to the ball game?" Theo asked.

"That is an aberration, the proverbial 'red herring' in all of this," Horace said firmly. "Much as I hate to disagree with you, Beatrix, that is a coincidence."

"In part, perhaps," she said slowly. "In turn, that means we should talk with Campbell and find out more about his excursion into Chicago." She turned to look towards the chain ferry. "I believe now would be a good time to do it. He will be back on this side by the time we arrive." She stood up, extended her hand toward Horace and asked, "Shall we?"

Fred enjoyed his guard duty at the hospital, beginning with the nurse assigned to keep watch over the patient in a private room. Fred wanted to know her name, how long she had been at the hospital, where she went to nursing school, and the name of who ran the kitchen. "You sound genuine, but I'm going to be watching to make sure no funny business happens." He walked over to close and lock the window, then pulled the drapes. When the nurse glared at him he said, "Might be sharpshooters out there, you know." The moment he left the room she opened the drapes and window.

He sat or stood outside the door, watching the hallway, and challenging anyone who came past him. When Doctor Landis heard complaints from his staff and patients' families, he went up on the ward to talk with Fred. "You could lighten up a little," he said. "You're making people jumpy."

"Just keeping an eye on things. It never hurts to be extra vigilant in times like these. You never know, someone could dress up like a nurse or orderly and try to get the jump on us and finish Cal off. Say, maybe we should have a password like we did when patrols would come back from a raid."

"I assume you're talking about the war?" Landis asked.

"Sure thing. We had a new password every day. Kept the Hun from trying to slip one over on us."

"I don't think we need to do that, do you?"

"Well, maybe not, but you can't be too careful."

"Just take it easy. Families that have someone here already have enough on their minds. Be gentle on them, understand?"

"Yes, Sir. Since you're the Commanding Officer of this outfit, you can count on me to obey orders," Fred said as he straightened up and saluted.

"By any chance did Chief Garrison say when he's sending up your replacement?" Landis asked with a slight tone of hopeful expectation.

"Nope. But don't you worry, I'll keep wide awake and eagle-eyed in case one of those thugs tries slipping in here. They're not getting past me, and that's for sure!"

"That's very reassuring," Landis sighed. "But listen, and this is an order. If things turn sour for him and the nurse calls for help, you keep out of the way. That happens, you let them do their work and don't slow them down."

"Yes, Sir. And I'll make sure the hallway stays clear, too!"

"Let's hope it doesn't happen," the physician said.

"Well, I'm doing my part. Me and God have been talking things over, and I've been bending His ear a little to pull Calvin through safe and sound. See, I grew up Methodist and I've been one my whole life. The preacher back home said God listens to us Methodists, and he must have been right on account of the fact I came home from France safe and sound."

"That's all the more reassuring. Very helpful, I'm sure. And remember something else. You're keeping guard duty, but don't stir things up. People will talk, and you know what they said about loose lips back during the war."

"Say, you got a good point, Doc. Thanks for reminding me. Undercover spy - that's what I'll do!"

"Well, carry on Sergeant," Doctor Landis said. "And keep it on the QT. We don't want to draw enemy fire."

"No, we sure don't want that. You can count on me, Sir."

Doctor Landis walked down the hall, rolling his eyes, and then realizing that Fred was still locked, at least part of the time, in the past decade during the war.

"Any luck?" Theo asked when his brother and Beatrix returned.

"None," Beatrix said flatly. "There was nothing more he could tell us, other than that he and his friends had planned the trip to Chicago several weeks earlier. Weather permitting, of course. So, there is little question that it was, as you said, an aberration, a red herring."

"Well, at least we know.," Theo said quietly.

"At least we know," Horace echoed. "And now we wait."

"Wait for what, Horace?" Beatrix asked.

Theo answered, "To see what Garrison can get out of the new bellhop." Both brothers saw Beatrix shiver at the thought of the methods the Chief might be using.

"I don't suppose either of you want to go over to the station and find out?" Horace asked. Neither Theo nor Beatrix responded.

To change the subject, Beatrix said, "Before all of this started, you were going to take a nap. You must be truly tired by now."

"Now that you mentioned it, yes and yes. Yes, I was going to take a nap, and yes, I am tired. I'm going to try again. Say, if I don't come up for dinner, just let me sleep, would you?"

"I am tired, also," Beatrix said. "I think I will join you." Realizing how her words could be misconstrued, she blushed and said, "In my own cabin, of course."

"Of course, Beatrix, of course," Theo teased.

"It's odd that Fred hasn't returned yet," Horace said just after sunset.

"Ah, he's probably at his post doing guard duty at the hospital. Either that, or he's out looking for those fellows with the touring car. I don't think there's anything to worry about. He can take care of himself," Theo said.

"Well, it's too nice a night not to enjoy a stroll. Anyone game for a walk?" Horace asked.

"I'd like to go with you, Grandfather," Phoebe said.

"I'm surprised you're not home in bed, young lady," he said.

"I'm staying on your boat with you again tonight. Aunt Clarice said I could, and so did mother, so, is it jake with you?" she asked.

"Jake, with me," he answered. "you're always a delight. Ice cream, and then straight to bed."

They had not gone far when Horace and Phoebe heard a "Phytt. Phytt," being hissed from the shadows. Horace paused, and the voice quietly said, "Abraham."

"Lincoln," Horace answered.

"I thought it looked like you, Doc, but I didn't want to take any chances. We got jumped right in our own headquarters! Get into the shadows and stay quiet, would you?"

CHAPTER TWENTY ONE

"See, I was relieved by one of Chief Garrison's boys, and decided to walk home on account of the fact that I'd been sitting so long I was getting a bit stiff where the pants meet the chair, if you know what and where I mean. I thought I ought to report back to the Chief that all was well and Doc Landis said Calvin was holding his own and there weren't no changes. Well, I got over here and it's a good thing I peeked in the window because there were a couple of rough-looking fellows with guns and the Chief with his hands up."

"Thunderation! What in the world is going on?"

"Well, it's like this you see. My platoon sergeant said that when Huns get you caught in a jam, to do the unexpected. So, it's like this. They had their back to the door, so I opened it real quiet-like and then slammed it shut just as hard as I could. That sure surprised them, and the Chief landed a punch on one of them hard as Dempsey. I opened the door again and fired off a round and the Chief got out faster than blue lightning."

"Where is he now? Did you wing one of them?" Horace asked.

"He's watching the front door in case they make a break for it. I think they're trying to get their man out of there, but the Chief's got the keys to the cells. We got 'em surrounded!"

"Well, maybe. Two of you, and the police station has got a case full of guns. They got more fire power than the two of you with pistols," Horace said. "That's hardly surrounding them, Fred."

"That's why I was mighty happy to see you, cause we've got to bring reinforcements up the line! If they come out shooting.....Well, let's hope they don't. I've been watching the back door and been thinking about what to do."

"Go on," Horace said gravely.

"Well, first thing is to get Miss Phoebe out of here on account of the fact that it might not be exactly safe. My thought is have her go back to the boat and tell Doc Theo we're in a tight corner. Now, if he was to put on his uniform and bring yours we'd have a couple of generals and that might get them to come to their senses toot and sweet."

"That's a fine idea. Two generals and no troops! Thunderation!" Horace growled.

"Well, I figured on you saying that. Now see, soon as you get into your uniform, one of you slip across over to the fire hall and ring the alarm. That'll bring everyone running, and then we got us an army!"

"There's a problem with that. That fire alarm will scare them and that's when they'll try to make a break for it, and an army's not much good without arms," Horace answered.

"Grandpa, I can run and tell Uncle Theo and then run down to the telephone. Miss Bobbie will still be there, and she can call all the firemen and tell them to bring their guns!" Phoebe said excitedly.

Both men were silent until Horace said, "That sounds a lot better than stirring up a ruckus. That fire alarm goes off and people will be coming out of the Big Pavilion like bats out of Carlsbad Cavern. All right, Phoebs, get going. Theo first, then get Bobbie on the switchboard and call up the reserves! Go. And when you get to Bobbie, tell her not to shut down the phone until she gets the all clear. And then you stay on the boat with Harriet and Clarice, is that clear? You are not to come back here, understand?"

"Yes, Sir, General!" she smiled as she saluted. The two men watched as she ran toward the *Aurora.*

"We were in the Medical Corp not the infantry! We don't know anything about soldiering!" Theo objected as he handed Horace his uniform. "You can come up with some crackpot ideas, you two, but this is the nuttiest of all."

Horace didn't answer, but quickly stripped down to his BVDs and stepped into his uniform. "Still fits!" he smiled.

"Now what?" Theo asked.

"Well, we got the Chief out in front, we're back here, so we got them surrounded. Any minute now the army will be coming," Horace said, enjoying Theo's frustration at his answers.

"A whole company of 'em!" Fred cackled.

"What army?" Theo demanded.

"Saugatuck's finest! The whole company of volunteer firemen. That army!"

"As you were little brother. As soon as they come, we'll take half the men and work our way around to the front and take our positions there. Fred, you deploy your men here in back and on both sides in case they try to make a break through the windows. Then we'll tell them to come out with their hands up. Ought to work, wouldn't you say, Sergeant?"

Theo stepped up to Horace and sniffed. "I don't smell anything, but you're sure acting like you're on giggle juice. What in the world is Beatrix doing here?" he asked, pointing to her walking in their direction.

As she drew closer, they could see she was carrying two medical bags. "Looks like the Medical Corp is moving up to the front," Fred said.

"Beatrix, pull back a bit and find someplace out of the line of fire in case we have casualties," Theo told her.

"Yes, Generals. Horace, you might need your walking stick," she said, handing it to him. She stepped up and gave him a quick kiss on the cheek. "You look good in uniform. Stay that way." She gave him another peck, then moved back a few yards behind an old carriage house.

"Now we wait," Horace said. "I'd better slip around in front and tell the Chief what we're doing."

"Yeah, I'm sure he'll be really happy to see you," Theo said in disgust. "Just real happy."

"When the fire brigade gets here we'll station half of them around the back and on the sides; the rest of them up here. If they make a run through the back, the men on the sides can lend a hand. My hope is that they come out with their hands up and no one gets hurt," Horace explained.

"That's your plan? Well, it just might work," the Chief said slowly in a tone of voice that revealed his doubts.

Within minutes the firemen were at their station house, in their gear, and ready. "We'd better take the truck with us," the fire captain said.

"You planning on flushing them out, Cap?" one of the men asked, laughing at his own joke.

"No, but that's not a bad idea. You three younger fellows, you weren't in the war, so I want you to get on the hose and be ready.

And keep your heads down, hear? Any shooting, and you get down and stay down. When we get in position, I want you to hook up the engine to the hydrant. And be quiet about it."

"Yes, Captain," one of them answered.

"And you," he said, pointing to a fireman still in high school. "You get up on that searchlight in case we need it."

"Captain, I'm good as the next man with a rifle," he objected. "And better than some."

"You just said the right word: Man. Look, I know you're good, but if something happens it's me that has to go see your folks. Now, you do as you're told."

"Looks like we've got a tank," Horace whispered to Chief Garrison.

"That's a fire truck in case you didn't know!" he snapped.

"Oh, I know a fire truck when I see one, but it's got a big water tank on it!" Horace teased. "Ready?"

"Much as I'll ever be. Say, you tell them not to start shooting unless I give the order. I don't want my place shot to bits and pieces, and don't forget we got that woman there."

"In one of the cells, I hope?" Horace asked.

"Yeah, with a solid steel door, but still...... and tell them to go easy with their axes, too."

Horace borrowed the fire captain's megaphone. "This is Brigadier General Horace Balfour, formerly of the American Expeditionary Force. My brother Brigadier General Theo Balfour is also present.

And with us is a company of well-armed infantry. You have one minute to come out with your hands up."

"Looks like a lot of old hicks playing fireman!" one of them mockingly shouted from inside the police station.

"Well those 'hicks' were in France during the war, so they're not going to be scared off by the likes of you. They know how to aim, shoot, and reload. Now, we do have one fellow with even more experience. Ener Ness here, fought with Grant in the Civil War. He's got a Henry Sixty-four. Takes a while to reload, but that sized ball will take down a buffalo. Ener, if those fellows don't come out with their hands up, you know what to do. Take your choice of targets."

"I sure do! Why, I'll blow them right back inside before they know they're knocking on the Pearly Gates. Not that St Pete's going to let him in!"

"Sure thing, old man!" one of the gunmen laughed.

Horace turned to the firemen. "First platoon load and aim. Safeties on."

From behind the station Theo shouted. "Second platoon, load and aim." He whispered, "Safeties on."

To Horace's surprise Theo was doing his part, playing along with the deception. "Medical Corp ready. Third squad is moving into position. You sharpshooters, get up those trees and get a bead on the windows. Medical Corp, make ready stretchers for the casualties!"

A familiar voice shouted, "How many stretchers, General?"

"Just two. There's only two of them," he shouted back, hoping the gunmen in the station heard him and understood the implications.

"They ought to be coming out any time," Chief Garrison said.

"Don't count on it," Horace told him. "Captain, order your men to turn that light around and aim it at the front of the building. Any chance you've got something to cut the power line? Our guests seem to be wasting a lot of electricity that's costing the village money."

"General, begging your pardon, but there's no need to cut the line. The main fuse box is just inside the steps down to the storm cellar. It's on the left half way down. One of my men can go around, slip down there and pull the shut-off," the fire captain said.

"Thunderation! Better idea," Horace agreed. "And say, you don't happen to have a can or two of motor oil on the truck do you?"

"Sure thing. You got something in mind, General?"

"I do. When your man turns off the light, I'd like that searchlight right on the front of the building. We'll send our compliments to them and blind them a little. Soon as we do that, have a man or two slip up to the front door and pour that oil on the sidewalk. I want them to make sure that door is unlocked and open just a bit The Chief should have the keys. Then get your men out of there and back behind the truck," Horace ordered.

"I see what you're up to. Guess we don't want any slip-ups do we, lessen its those two fellows inside," the captain laughed.

"Right," Horace said. "Now, once your fellows are back here, turn that hose on the door and give them a blast."

"That might not work if they barred the door," Chief Garrison interrupted.

"Glad you told me. That plan might not work. Well, if it doesn't, we'll improvise. If they barred the door, we'll have to bust it down," Horace said slowly. He spotted their Buick sitting across the street. "Captain, you'll need to pull your truck up a few feet so we've got a straight shot up the sidewalk with our battering ram. That car is heavy enough to do that job."

"You can't do that!" the Chief objected.

"It's that or a gunfight," Horace told him. "You don't want that. First shot and you'll have half the town down here to see what's going on. And then we're going to need more than a couple of stretchers."

"I see your point, but I want you to know I don't like it."

"I understand. I don't especially like it either, so let's see if we can't get them to come out before that happens. Captain, send your man around to douse the lights. Chief, we'll need your keys."

It took a couple of minutes to get everyone in position and ready.

Theo agreed with the plan and ordered two men to help open the doors leading down to the storm cellar. The hinges were rusty, and when two of the firemen opened the door they screeched and echoed. One of the men lost his grip on the door and it fell back into place, making a loud bang. "All right you men, get your charges ready. Soon as I give the order, light the fuses and toss them down the cellar!" he shouted. Quickly he ran his right hand under his chin, making a slicing motion over his throat, letting the rest of his men know not to move.

"Hold up, General," Fred whispered. "Couple of you fellows find a rock or bucket or anything to throw down there. Make a little noise and rattle them but good!"

Theo nodded in agreement.

The lights went out, and several men threw their rocks into the basement, at least one of them hitting the furnace. It rattled and banged, echoing up through the ducts and grate into the main floor.

"Now!" Horace shouted to the men in the front.

The fire captain shouted, "Jim, swing that light around!"

CHAPTER TWENTY TWO

The intense light covered the windows and front door and two of the firemen slipped in close along the front, keeping low to the ground. "That's Bob Campbell," Horace whispered to the Chief and Captain. "He's on the brigade?"

"Sure is," the captain said proudly. "Nice to see him breaking into the jail instead of the other way around."

They watched as he knelt to the side of the front door, slipped the key in the lock and opened it a fraction of an inch, then pulled back. With a nod to the fireman on the other side, both of them poured their can of oil onto the sidewalk, making sure it was well coated. They quickly retreated and came back to the truck.

With a wave of his hand and motion toward the front door, the Chief let the men on the hose know it was time to give the front a blast. Water arched across the small front lawn and hit the door, forcing it open, and flooding the first floor.

"My office!" Chief Garrison wailed. "You're soaking everything. It's getting soaked!"

"That usually happens when you use water," the Captain said quietly. "Nothing beats a two inch hose in a town with good water pressure." He signalled the men to turn off the water.

Garrison recovered from his shock and shouted. "This is police chief Garrison. I've got a full platoon with their guns trained on you, and more men on their way. That's a lot of fire power, and I wouldn't mind cutting you to ribbons. So, come out with your hands up!" He turned and shouted up to Ener, "Get that buffalo gun ready. One of them makes a false move and plug him!"

"Got my finger on the trigger, Chief! All I have to do is pull the hammer back and let him have it."

There was no answer from inside. "Another burst from the hose!" the fire captain ordered. "Front door and windows. Give them something to think about."

"You men with the grenades, standby!" Horace shouted, then shook his head to let the fire captain and Chief Garrison he was bluffing. "Hose!"

The firemen opened the hose a second time, shattering the window on the left, then the right, and flooding the building with more water for twenty seconds.

"You come to your senses yet, or you want to get blown to bits?" Horace shouted through the megaphone.

There was an uncomfortably long pause, and finally someone inside shouted. "Don't shoot! Don't shoot! We're coming out!"

"Make sure your hands are where I can see them, or so help me, we will shoot!" Garrison shouted.

"We hear you. We're coming out. Don't shoot! Don't shoot!"

"Watch 'em, men," Horace ordered.

Slowly, cautiously, the two thugs came to the front door, hands raised. They stopped. "We're unarmed. Don't shoot!" one of them pleaded.

"Get out here, now!" the chief ordered.

Both of them stepped across the threshold, and instantly slipped and fell on the oil and water on the sidewalk.

"Get 'em!" the Chief shouted.

A dozen men charged forward, each wanting the bragging rights of catching a Chicago gangster. It was a melee as the firemen began slipping, grabbing for each other and the gunmen, and falling down. Fists were flying, and the men were shouting at each other.

Fred and Theo, along with the rest of the men from town hurried around to the front. Two of the younger men jumped into the fray, while the Balfours and Fred doubled up laughing. Realizing that the danger was over, Beatrix ran to join them. For a moment she said nothing, then joined in the laughter until tears came down her face.

"Is anyone hurt?" she finally asked between laughs.

"Not yet, but if this keeps up much longer there are going to be some black eyes by morning," Horace said, roaring with laughter. "Look at them go at it. Looks like a football game in the mud."

"Ener, discharge your weapon. High and over the river toward the woods!" the chief ordered.

"Yes, Sir. With pleasure!"

He stood up, aimed, pulled back the hammer and touched the trigger. Nothing happened. He tried a second time with the same result. From a small pouch he pulled out a percussion cap and placed it on the nipple. "Third time's the trick!" he shouted. It was. The shot echoed off the front of the police station and through the town.

"That's enough!" the Chief shouted. "Save some so they can get the chair!"

The men gradually obeyed, two of them slipping and skating on the sidewalk as they tried to stand. The fire captain responded quickly, "Couple of you men get the sand buckets down here and give us some traction. Garrison will want to lock those two up."

Chief Garrison looked in dismay at the lobby of his police station. The wanted posters and announcements on a wall were soaked, and ink was running down from them. Papers had been pushed aside and spread across the floor. The electric light on his desk had shattered on the floor, and his chair had been pushed by the water into a corner. He shook his head. "This is a real mess," he moaned.

"Yeah, but you got the two killers, didn't lose your prisoners, and let's face it, the place needed a good cleaning," Horace told him. From the corner of his eye he could see Beatrix still trying to stifle a giggle and regain her composure.

"Yeah, yeah, yeah," the Chief moaned. "We gotta get someone to board up those windows and clean the place."

Together with a deputy and a few others, the prisoners were ushered into the cells in the back room. "Looks like you got company," he announced as he unceremoniously shoved them into the cage with the bellhop. "You can keep each other company."

"Hey, you can't leave us like this. We're soaked to the skin and dirty," one of them objected.

"Yeah, you sure are. Too bad about that, too." He sniffed the air. "And you don't smell so good. I hope you didn't slip on something. Mrs. Wilson's dog hangs around here most of the time, and he's got stomach trouble. Don't worry, a week from yesterday the laundry service will be here. The Chief smiled when the bellhop tried to move further away. He locked the door, and then unlocked Miss Randall's cell, looked to make certain she was all right, and locked it again. As he left the back room he turned and said, "Nitey-nite boys. Sleep tight and don't let the bed bugs bite."

"Well Chief, we'll leave you to it. My brother and I and probably Fred and Doctor Howell have had enough excitement for one night," Horace said, extending his right hand.

"Say, you don't want to help clean up the place, do you?" he asked.

"That is very kind of you to offer, Chief Garrison," Beatrix said, "but I believe we should stay out of your way."

"I found it quite exhilarating," Beatrix said as she walked with Horace and Theo, holding their arms. "It made me realize that I have never once danced with a general in uniform," she nodded toward the Big Pavilion.

"You're with two generals," Theo reminded her.

"Yes, two generals. And since we are all chaperoning one another, I shall hope for one dance with each of you. And you, too, Fred.

"Thank you just the same, Doc, but on account of the fact that I'm a Methodist and we Methodists don't think any too highly of dancing...." Fred answered.

"I understand," Beatrix said. "Gentlemen, one Fox Trot each."

CHAPTER TWENTY THREE

Four days later Chief Garrison walked up the gangplank on the *Aurora* in search of Horace and Beatrix. "Come to pin a medal on us, or give us a commendation from the governor?" Horace asked brightly.

"Ah, go on. I got a puzzler of a letter from the mayor of Chicago," the chief said, handing it to Horace, who read it and without comment, handed it to Beatrix. When she finished, she returned it to the Chief and asked his intentions.

"Well, it doesn't make a lot of sense. You saw what he wrote. He'd take it as a personal favor if I would turn over those two thugs. At least I got their names thanks to the mayor: Pete and Frank Gutzman. He said he'd send some of his officers to take them off my hands."

"I got that part," Horace said. "So, what are you going to do?"

"I've never had a big city mayor wanting to do anything like that. Maybe he figures that our jail isn't strong enough to hold them or something, so he wants to do me a favor. In a way, it sort of makes sense, the mayor taking him off my hands. If these two fellows have friends or are part of some gang, they might come up here to bust them out, and we might not get so lucky the next time. It doesn't make a lot of sense, but the way I figure it, he's offering to do us a favour, like I said."

"Have you told anyone about this letter?" Horace asked.

"Nope, just you two," the Chief answered.

"Let's keep it that way for a while longer while we think this over," Horace answered, pulling out his pipe. "I take it you're holding the bellhop and Miss Randall, too?"

"Got them all on ice."

"Let's keep it that way, and keep a guard on Cal, too. Doctor Landis said he seems to be improving, but he's still under sedation. We saw him just an hour or so ago. He's stable, but he's going to be in a lot of pain for the long haul," Horace said.

"Yeah, I was just up to the hospital to have a look-see, and Doc Landis told me the same thing." He stood up to leave. "Soon as you come up with an idea about that letter, let me know, would you?"

"You get anything out of the bellhop?" Horace asked.

"Not a peep. I can't even get a name out of him. He's in a heap of trouble with the list of charges I'm holding him on. And if Cal passes, then it's going to be first-degree murder. Makes me wish I could give him the electric chair, hurting a nice fellow like Calvin that way."

"Perhaps you could get a small section of rubber hose at Koening's," Beatrix suggested. Horace looked shocked, not knowing if she was serious or not.

"Got one already for special occasions, and I'm just of a mind to use it on him until he sings," the chief said, also uncertain if she was serious. It was out of character for her. "Say, tell me how you think they did it, Doctor Balfour, murdering someone and stuff him into the box on the chain ferry?"

"Bob thought there was just one man, but since you're holding two, and they have that big brown Buick, likely as not they killed Haggerty. I don't think Bob saw the other one that night. Don't forget, the driver kept Bob busy talking to him, his back to the car the whole time. I figure the second one slipped out of the backseat, dragged Haggerty's body out and put him in the box and locked it. Good thing that Bob didn't notice anything."

"How do you figure that?" the Chief asked.

"Those two are professional killers. Bob would have been in the box, too."

Beatrix gasped in horror.

Horace and Beatrix went into his study and closed the door. "Do you know anything about this William Thompson?" Horace asked.

"Only that he is the mayor of Chicago, and quite a dashing-looking man."

"Well, Big Bill as his friends call him, is about as crooked as they come. He never saw a bribe he didn't like and always holds out his hand for more. Capone and Morgan both pay him to turn a blind eye to the rackets. I figure he's playing one of them off against the other to keep the money coming in."

Beatrix said nothing, staring off into the distance, and Horace knew it meant she was thinking. He waited.

"Very likely, this is not the generous offer it seems," Beatrix said. "If what you say is accurate, perhaps Mr. Moran slid some money to the mayor to get his men back. Or, Mr. Capone slid some money to the mayor so he could get his hands on his rival's gunmen.

"It's a crooked scheme whichever way you look at it. It's beyond me that the Chief could be so naive as to not see it. Maybe there was more in that envelope than a letter - cash."

"What about the bellhop, then?" Beatrix asked. "Why doesn't the mayor care about him?"

"He came out of Detroit. I keep reading in the papers about a gang over on the east side of the state. I think they're the Purple

Gang, and rumor has it that Moran hires some of them to do his dirty work for him - killings, things like that. Probably Capone, too. But Big Bill wouldn't care about him. And you notice that there's no interest in Miss Randall, either. Just these two thugs. I'll bet they're a real disappointment to their mother, the way they turned out," Horace said flatly.

"Please tell me you have an idea," Beatrix said. "Wait! If the mayor didn't mention Miss Randall, perhaps it means she had nothing to do with any of it."

"Not yet. As Holmes would tell Watson, 'this is a three-pipe case.'" Horace pulled out the pipe in his jacket pocket, two more from his desk, and another one off the shelf. He looked at her and said, "I'm not as smart as Holmes. This might take four or more."

"You are too polite to ask me to leave, so I'll take this opportunity to let you think," Beatrix said.

Four hours later Horace came out on deck, leaving the door to his study open. "Let's talk," he told Beatrix. She listened and in the end said, "It might work. Off to see the Chief? He nodded.

"Well, no, I haven't got any reason to hold Miss Randall. Those two mugs out of Chicago keep saying she's nothing but a patsy. Sure, I can let her go. I'd just as soon get her out of here as anything else," Garrison said. "Doesn't seem quite proper to have a woman locked up in the same jail as men."

"Unconditional release?" Horace asked.

"Sure, why not? I got no reason to hold her," the Chief answered. "Now, what do I do about the two brothers?"

"To use your phrase, keep them on ice for a couple more days before you write to the mayor. If he calls or puts the pressure on, tell him his letter is being reviewed by the county attorney. Tell him anything. Just stall."

"Well, I guess, if you say so, but I still think the whole situation is shady, and you're not shedding much light on it," the Chief moaned. "I'll have her ready to go when you get back here."

"Now what?" Beatrix asked as they walked back to the boat.

"We pack overnight bags and go into Chicago. And we're taking Miss Randall along with us."

Beatrix said nothing. A quarter hour later, they were ready to leave.

"Look, you got every reason to be sore with us, and I'm sorry about the way we leaned on you," Horace started to apologize to Miss Randall.

"Leaned. Scared me half to do, is more like it! Regular giving a girl the third degree, and me not deserving it!" she retorted. "Accusing me of murder and counterfeiting and saying I'd get sent to the pen like that!"

"That was how we knew you were telling the truth. And we had you locked up because it was safer than anywhere else," Beatrix added. "You know who was in the cells next to you?"

"No,"

"One of them is a hired killer from Detroit. You remember that bellhop at the hotel? Well, he nearly killed him. And the others were a couple of Mr. Moran's worst killers - Frank and Pete Guzman. How do you like those rotten apples?" Beatrix asked.

"We're going into Chicago on the train. You'll be safe with us getting to Chicago. And then we're putting you on the Southwest Chief to California. It's a one-way ticket. You wanted a chance to be an actress in Hollywood, well, it's the best offer we can make. Go out there and be a star, if you can. We're paying for the ticket, and want you to have this." He handed her an envelope full of cash. "Don't worry, there aren't any twenties."

"You might take some time to consider changing your name," Beatrix added.

"Sure, I could do that. My real name is Sally Radjokowitz and I shortened it. I can change it again, real easy like."

They waited in the Great Hall for Sally Randall's train to be announced, said their goodbyes, and left the station. "See you on screen in the movie palace," Horace said.

"I thought we were returning home," Beatrix said.

"I didn't want to tell you earlier. One more stop," he said when they walked out of Union Station onto the street. Horace hailed a taxi, and Beatrix gasped when she heard him tell the driver, "Tribune Tower." She paled slightly.

"Welcome to Chicagoland's Tribune Tower," the receptionist at the desk greeted them. "Do you have an appointment with someone."

"No. I'm here to see Colonel McCormick," Horace said firmly.

"I'm sorry, but the colonel doesn't see anyone without an appointment," she smiled.

"Please tell his secretary that it is Brigadier General Horace Balfour of the AEF Medical Corp and Doctor Beatrix Howell to see him. And please tell the colonel that my late son James Balfour served under his command at Cantigny, and later worked for the paper until....." his voice trailed off and he choked up.

The receptionist gasped, raising her hand up to her mouth. "He was a reporter here, wasn't he? I just talked with Mr. Lindal's secretary and she mentioned him not two hours ago. Oh, I am so sorry. Let me see what I can do. I know the colonel is still in the building."

She telephoned to the owner's office and whispered. "There's a '75' here by the name of General Balfour. Brigadier General Balfour."

The receptionist put down the phone and jotted a quick note. "Give this to the elevator operator. Someone will meet you on his floor."

"Horace, are you sure about this? Beatrix whispered.

"Yup." He said, his voice slightly quaking. To his surprise, she brushed the back of her hand against his, then held it, squeezed, and let go.

Horace and Beatrix were ushered into the colonel's office, and the two men stood at attention to salute each other. "What can I do for you, General?" McCormick asked, directing them to chairs across his desk.

"You're the one man who can handle this. You're a busy man, so I'll come straight to the point. Big Bill is a crook and we both know it. The police are on the take, so are most of the aldermen...." Horace started. "Probably the prosecutors, as well."

"All the way down to the precinct level and back up again. A kid wants a job on the back of a garbage wagon and the old man has to make a financial contribution. Small stuff compared to the gangs, but you are correct. The mayor is corrupt. Tell me something I don't know, General."

For the next few minutes Horace explained about the counterfeit money, the murder, the Guzman brothers, and the arrest of a gunman from the Purple Gang. "And on top of it, your mayor would like our police chief to hand them over. Now, do you figure it's Moran paying off the mayor to get them back, or Capone paying him to shoot them before they get to the Indiana state line? You're the only man who can stop this. You're bigger and more powerful than all of them. You've been crusading against those vermin like you did against the Hun."

The truth and flattery seemed to be working.

"Leave it to me, general," the colonel said. "We'll turn the power of the press on them and squeeze hard. I've got a good reporter covering the crime beat. Jake, ah, ah, Jake Lindal. He's a good man. A real straight arrow. Don't worry, the Guzmans won't get away with it. They'll get what they deserve. My word, one officer to another." He stood up from his desk.

"You have a plan, I hope?" Beatrix asked.

The colonel flashed her a smile. "I'll put in a call to the State Police. The mayor doesn't control them. You have your police send them down here and call me. I'll have the police waiting for them the moment they cross over from Indiana. And I'll have Jake and a photographer there to do a piece for my paper. Front page, top of the fold. Nothing I like better than to lob a whiz bang over to City Hall!" He walked around his desk to where Horace and Beatrix were now standing.

"Colonel McCormick, perhaps you will have the opportunity to accompany your reporter when the prisoners are handed over to the State Police. A photograph of you along with the story would let everyone know that you take a personal interest in fighting corruption. Perhaps it could catapult you right into the White House," Beatrix said quietly.

To Horace's amusement, Colonel McCormick pulled himself up to full height. "That is something to consider," he told her. Her flattery worked.

Colonel McCormick turned to Horace and said, "There's something I want you to know. I had a lot of good junior officers over there in France, but none finer than your boy. And a lot of good reporters here at the paper, but if he hadn't been in the wrong place at the wrong time, your boy would have been winning the Pulitzer Prize for reporting. I told him to be careful but he said it was his job to report the news. He was killed in action, doing his duty to tell the truth to our readers. You and I'd be happier men if he hadn't been so headstrong."

"Courageous," Horace corrected him. "Thank you, Colonel."

"You take care of him. He's a good man," McCormick told Beatrix.

On the elevator ride down the tower Beatrix whispered. "A bit patronizing, but on the whole, I absolutely agree - you are a very good man."

"How about that taking care of me part?" Horace asked carefully.

"I think that might be a very good idea."

When they were once again on Michigan Avenue, Horace looked at his watch. "Seems to me that we have about four hours to kill before the train home. How about something to eat at the new place, the Allerton Hotel? I heard they have a nice little restaurant up on the top floor."

"Let's throw caution to the wind and do it." Beatrix smiled. "I'm not fond of heights, you know."

"Beatrix! You fly an aeroplane, remember?" Horace objected.

"That, Doctor Balfour, is entirely different!" she giggled.

"Glad you said that. I've got something I've been wanting to talk over with you for a long time."

Beatrix shivered slightly, drew in her breath and swallowed.

Coming soon:
The Murder at Nine Finger Charlie's Art Emporium.

Made in the USA
Middletown, DE
27 July 2019